Passion at the Palais Royal

Bleu Blanc Rogue
Book 3

Delphine Roy

Dearest Reader;

Thank you for your support of a small press. At Dragonblade Publishing, we strive to bring you the highest quality Historical Romance from some of the best authors in the business. Without your support, there is no 'us', so we sincerely hope you adore these stories and find some new favorite authors along the way.

Happy Reading!

CEO, Dragonblade Publishing

Chapter One

Paris, December 1802

"How lucky to run into you tonight, *monsieur*."

A delicate hand ran up Nicolas Lefevre's arm, and he glanced over his shoulder. A slight woman clad in a low-cut chartreuse gown gazed up at him. A turban that matched her dress was arranged on auburn ringlets, and her eyes sparkled with mischief.

Hortense. Good Lord, he hadn't seen her in weeks, but somehow the crush of people in the lobby of the Opéra Comique had managed to bring some pleasant company his way.

He smiled and touched the tip of his hat. "Madame de Vijeux. A lucky meeting indeed."

She slipped her hand into the crook of his arm and fluttered her feathered fan. "It feels wrong for you to address me so formally. Especially after—"

He cleared his throat. "Manners, my dear. We are in public."

They shouldered through the crowd, surrounded on all sides by dark evening coats, glinting brocade dresses and tasseled cashmere shawls. A chandelier hanging from the dome bathed the hall in a golden glow. Music, light, a cacophony of voices and a comely lady at his arm. More than enough to make him forget how bitterly cold it was outside.

Hortense nodded left and right to greet people she knew. "I doubt anyone present gives a toss about my reputation. I have worked hard to earn it, after all."

"And I am honored to have contributed to your effort."

Indeed, of all the merry widows of Paris, Hortense was probably the merriest, and made no attempt to hide it.

"That's all well and good, Nicolas, but I'll have you know I am very cross with you," she scolded. "You have not once come to see me since October!"

"I heard you had taken up with someone," he defended himself. "Some young barrister or other."

"Oh yes, Hadrien. He's here with me, but I lost him when we left my box for the intermission." They stopped for a moment, and she rose on tiptoes, stretching her neck. "This crowd, my God, it's never been worse! Of course, they've all come to hear Madame Saint Yves sing in *Cosi Fan Tutte*. Isn't she splendid?"

"Actually, I know her quite well…"

Before he could explain any further, something, or rather *someone*, caught his attention. A young woman sashaying down the staircase, accompanied by a tall man with dark hair and a pointed nose. The man looked familiar, but Nicolas couldn't place him. The woman, though…

She glanced in his direction, and their gazes met. Only an instant, for she looked away immediately, but it was enough to make a sliver of heat stir in his chest.

Her eyes were striking, large and deep and the palest blue, like frost. Her neck was slender, and her oval face was framed with soft, light brown waves. The dark slashes of her brows stood out in contrast to those blue eyes, heavier than most women wore them, but somehow they added an expressive sensuality to her face, balancing a set of plump lips.

"An acquaintance of yours, or are you just enjoying the view?" Hortense teased, following his gaze toward the couple.

He smiled. "An evening at the opera is sure to bring out all the most beautiful women of Paris. But no, I don't know her. Nor him, as a matter of fact."

As soon as the words left his mouth, an unsettled feeling replaced the sliver of heat. A friend of Hortense came to greet them, but as they chatted, Nicolas continued to observe the couple. People came to the opera to socialize, yet this pair had not spoken a word to anyone, nor to each other. Their clothes were certainly elegant and well-made—a perfectly cut wool jacket over a crimson waistcoat for him, a steely blue gown for her that cinched her slim waist. And she, in particular, carried herself with the sort of easy grace only bestowed on those born in wealth. Chin held high, shoulders back, step so soft it was almost as if she was floating instead of walking.

Why, then, did he get the impression that the two of them were playacting? And at what, for that matter?

Irrational, perhaps. But his instincts seldom set him on the wrong foot, and he'd seen more than enough petty thievery in his day to sense when someone was looking for a mark.

They were careful not to draw attention, and indeed, no one paid them any heed as they moved slowly on the edge of the crowd. Easier to get away than in the middle of a throng.

The young man bumped into a portly gentleman wearing a silk scarf over his coat. He then made a show of apologizing and picked up something from the ground—a small silver flask. Then handed it back to the man.

The corner of Nicolas's mouth tilted up. Of course. Nothing like a fake display of honesty to distract a mark while your partner picked his pockets. The young woman's sleight of hand was so nimble and discreet that Nicolas barely saw her arm move under her shawl.

Oh, she was good. *Very* good.

"If you'll excuse me, *mesdames*," he told Hortense and her friend. "I'll be back in just a moment."

The couple moved on, picking up the pace ever so slightly. Then they separated. Nicolas followed the young woman into the mirrored gallery that ran all the way to the side exit of the Opéra Comique.

He lengthened his stride. Why was he even chasing her? He was hardly a vigilante. This was Paris, after all. Pockets would get picked, purses cut, and wealthy patrons robbed when all they wanted was a night's worth of entertainment.

But *her*... She was unlike any thief he'd ever seen. Skilled, certainly, but not a *grisette*, a young working woman hardened by the streets.

Who the devil had put her up to this?

The crowd was sparser here, mostly couples, heads bent toward each other, engaged in an intimate conversation. With some luck, people would just assume he was trying to catch up with his sweetheart after a spat.

The young woman tensed, as if she'd sensed his presence. She didn't so much as glance behind her, but her feet moved faster. No matter, he'd catch up before she reached the door.

She was going as fast as she could short of running. Closer now... One, two, three steps, and he grasped her wrist.

She halted. Turned. And kicked him right in the shin.

"*Sacredieu*," he cursed, but didn't release her.

"Unhand me immediately," she growled, "or I'll scream."

She flailed against him, tried to kick him again. Good Lord, what a wildcat. He loosened his grip just enough to turn her around and press her arm against her back. Against him. He tightened his fingers around her thin wrist, and she stilled.

"Quiet now, *madame*," he murmured against her hair. "I know what you have in your reticule. If you scream, you'll end the evening in a holding cell at the *gendarmerie*."

Her pulse beat against his fingers, and her body trembled, like a bird fluttering against the bars of a cage. "Take it. I don't care. Just let me go."

"That's not what I came for. Who's your employer? You must be working for someone. This is Chardon's sector, but his gang doesn't usually work *inside* the opera."

"Let me go," she protested. "*Please.*"

The sudden desperation in her voice made him hesitate. If she was being coerced…

A loud bell rang out. Half a second, and his grip slackened. She elbowed him with all her strength, broke free and dashed away, only glancing back at him before opening the door. An inrush of biting air swept through the corridor, but it vanished just as quickly as she did when the door slammed shut.

Damn it to hell. All those years undefeated at *savate*, and that wisp of a woman had thrown him off balance.

It must be her eyes. Her eyes had landed the first blow, and he hadn't stood a chance.

Nicolas sighed and made his way back to the main hall. The bell rang again to signal the end of intermission.

"Nicolas, over here!"

Hortense was waving at him. She'd found her barrister, but the same inviting light animated her eyes nonetheless. Why limit yourself to one act when you could enjoy two?

He nodded, yet returned to his box alone. Cold as it was, he didn't feel like warming anyone's bed tonight.

VIOLETTE COVERED HER hair with her toque and wrapped her shawl around her shoulders, clutching at the edges. Light wool, soft and warm, just as fine as anything she'd worn in her youth, but it didn't help. Her limbs trembled, her knees were weak, her face both heated and prickling with cold.

No time to stop and take a breath. She must hurry. Who knew how long it would take their mark to realize his purse was missing?

And if that other man came after her…

She glanced back behind her. No one. He'd stayed inside the opera house, whoever he was. She'd only had time to make out his most distinct features: curly red-gold hair, brilliant green eyes, a tall frame, a long nose. And his voice, of course. Deep, steady, poised. Almost nonchalant, even as he questioned her. As if catching a pickpocket in the act at the opera was an ordinary occurrence for him.

How on earth had he spotted her when she'd taken such care to go unnoticed? She'd done this countless times in the past few months and had never once been caught. Why tonight, and why him?

She shook the questions away. Curiosity was a luxury she simply couldn't afford at the moment.

Two streets north, and she spotted the waiting fiacre. She tapped on the door—one time, twice, then once more—and it opened. She slid inside.

"Splendid. Right on time."

Jacques Lenoir watched her keenly under his dark brow as she took a seat across from him. With his chestnut hair and broad shoulders, she supposed one could qualify him as handsome, but something in his gaze made her skin crawl. Something rapacious and arrogant that he tried to hide with a smile.

"I left just as the second intermission was ending," she said.

"I trust you were successful?"

She nodded and fished the purse from her reticule, handing it to him, along with a pair of silver opera glasses and a pearl bracelet. Lenoir weighed the loot in his palm and his smile broadened.

"You really have a rare talent, dear Violette. The Boneman will be pleased."

The Boneman. Did he even have a real name? She'd heard all sorts of rumors about him. That he lived in the catacombs and never came out by the light of day. That he carried a necklace fashioned out of teeth around his neck. Even if they were nonsense, the man must be fearsome indeed to rule over half the thugs of Paris. She shivered and stared out the window so as not to meet Lenoir's eye.

"How long must we wait for Bravard?"

"Another minute, and if he doesn't show, we leave." He reached out to take her hand in his. "I imagine you must be in a hurry to go to bed after a night's work."

It took everything in her power not to snatch her hand away. Since she'd started working for the Boneman's organization, Lenoir had established himself as her protector of sorts. Or so he claimed. Odious as he may be, if she crossed him, someone far worse might take his place.

She harbored no illusions on Lenoir. The only reason he had not yet taken his so-called *protection* to her bedroom was because his master held him on too tight a leash. But better a dog on a leash than one in the wild.

"Yes, I am rather tired," she said, relaxing her hand against his.

Though home would not provide the type of rest she truly needed. No matter. The oblivion of sleep called to her.

A series of knocks resounded through the cabin. Lenoir released her hand and opened the door.

Bravard stepped inside.

"Bloody awful time getting out of that shithole," he grumbled in the rough, thick accent of the Parisian streets. "More crowded than the dead queen's cunt. Can't you send me somewhere other than among those fucking nobs?"

He shot her a dark glare. *Fucking nobs.* She had belonged to that class once, in a past that wasn't so distant, though it felt like several lifetimes ago. But for people like Bravard, her birth was a stain she would never erase, no matter how dire her current situation was, and no matter how good she was at picking pockets.

Lenoir thumped his fist against the ceiling, and the fiacre rattled off. "You know how to change your voice and talk as if your whore of a mother popped you out on silk sheets, not in the gutter. It's a useful skill to have."

Bravard crossed his arms over his chest. "Your mother wasn't any less of a whore. You're just better at licking the Boneman's arse."

"Quiet. You'll do as I tell you. You two make an efficient team. That's quite a haul you got brought in, and no one was the wiser."

Violette tapped her fingers on her thigh. No telling how badly Lenoir would react if he found out she'd been caught.

Caught and released. The man was strong, sharp, with lightening quick reflexes. Why had he hesitated and loosened his grip on her at that moment?

She didn't even know his name. Not that she was in any rush to find out.

Chapter Two

VIOLETTE OPENED HER eyes to darkness. For a few moments, she stared at the crack between the velvet draperies at the bleak, gray dawn that was only starting to lighten the sky. She had managed to salvage those draperies, despite her brother's insistence on selling them. They couldn't have gotten much out of them, worn as they were. Besides, once winter came, they'd needed something to prevent frigid drafts from blowing between the cracks of the window frame. The cold would have been their death.

Lord have mercy, it was cold enough as it was. She curled up under the covers, wanting nothing more than to lose herself in sleep again, to feel warm and safe if only for a few hours. But she must get up, get dressed, try to find food, report to Lenoir for further orders.

She rose and pulled the ends of a wool shawl around her chest, holding it in place as well as she could while she washed with the icy water left in her porcelain basin. That, too, she had managed to hold onto, though the chest of drawers was gone, and she had to leave the basin on the floor. When she finally undressed to slip on her underclothes, gooseflesh erupted on her skin and her teeth chattered. The wooden floor was hard and chilled as stone under her feet.

A fire in every room. Lush carpets on the ground. Steaming hot dishes ready and waiting on the table. All of those luxuries she had known in the past and taken for granted, young as she had been. When her family had been forced to relocate from their estate in a much smaller house—little better than a cottage, really—during the Revolution, her parents still had the funds to maintain a comfortable lifestyle. And even when her uncle had taken her and Emile in after their parents' death, there was still money enough for two domestics, firewood, and hearty meals.

Now, the only thing left of the vast De la Roque fortune was the roof over their head and the walls surrounding them, which they'd inherited from their uncle. Violette opened her trunk and took out a wine-colored dress, the warmest she owned. She had hemmed it over and over, but it was threadbare in places. What would happen when she could no longer wear it?

You know what will happen. Or rather who will offer to buy you a new one.

She shook her head. No, none of that now. Each day brought its own trouble.

She stepped out of her room. The flat was entirely silent. Unsurprising, she didn't expect Emile to be up at this hour. She made her way to the dining room and found half of a loaf of bread left on the table. She sat down to tear off a piece. It was tough, and barely enough to calm her growling stomach. A hot drink. Butter. Oh, butter, smooth and thick and creamy…

Lenoir might invite her to have luncheon with him if she got to the café early enough. Would it be so wrong to accept, just this once?

She tore off another piece of bread. She would have to make inventory of what was left of their sparse furnishings. Maybe something might fetch a few francs.

A knock came from the front door. Violette jumped to her feet, her heart giving a painful lurch. Slowly, she advanced toward the front hall. The knock came again.

"Who's there?"

"I'm here to clean," came a woman's voice from the other side of the door. "Monsieur Lenoir sent me."

Violette hesitated only a moment before opening. A young woman in a plain dark dress, cheeks red from the cold, stood in waiting with a broom and a bucket.

"You say Lenoir sent you?"

The young woman nodded. "Yes. Asked me to light the fires as well."

"I can do that myself." Though they only had enough firewood left for one.

"As you wish, *mademoiselle*. I'm at your service for any task that needs doing. And I'm no cook but I can make simple dishes."

Violette sighed. Lenoir must have heard they'd let go of their last domestic two weeks prior. And now he was sending someone to keep tabs on her, make sure she didn't flee in the middle of the night.

But where would she even go? To say nothing of Emile. He was barely in any state to walk down the stairs, though that certainly didn't stop him when he was out looking for intoxicating drink.

"Very well," she finally said, and stepped aside to let the girl in. "I suppose this place could use a good scrubbing."

The young woman went to work immediately. Violette tiptoed down the corridor to her brother's room. That, too, needed a thorough cleaning, more than that poor girl could possibly imagine. But there was the problem of actually getting her brother out of there.

She slowly opened the door and peeked inside. The stench of stale sweat, soiled sheets, and alcohol rushed to her nostrils, so pungent she nearly gagged. Emile lay on the bed in his shirt and breeches, limbs spread across the mattress, hair disheveled. No even a blanket over him. How was he not freezing?

An empty bottle lay on the ground beside the bed. There was her answer. She'd heard him staggering into the house in the middle of the night, talking to himself, and then slamming the door shut behind him. At least he'd made it this far before he passed out.

How in the devil did he find the money for liquor? To what depths did he sink? She couldn't bear to think of it. But underlying her despair was anger. Pure, white-hot anger that made her want to shake and slap him.

Damn him. Damn him to hell. If it weren't for his debts…

She slammed the door shut again. She'd tell the girl not to bother for now. Let him sleep on his soiled sheets while she went and asked Lenoir if she could work tonight.

She wouldn't stoop to begging. Not yet, and not for food or clothes. But repaying Emile's debts to the Boneman left her so little money that soon she'd have no choice.

THUMP.

The man hit the floor of the ring and a splatter of blood burst from his lips. The referee started counting.

"Come on, damn you," Nicolas muttered, his fists curled tightly. The crowd was tightly packed around the makeshift ring, moving and roaring as one like a wild animal out for the kill, but he stood on a bench further in the back to have a clearer view of the fight.

Four… five… six…

He focused on Boutin, who loomed over his felled opponent, panting heavily, his hair slick with sweat over his brow. Four more seconds, and he would win it all.

Nine… ten…

"The match goes to Boutin," the arbiter called.

A cheer rose from several gentlemen in the audience. Nicolas uncurled his hands to break out in a loud clap. *Sacredieu*, it had been a close bout, but his student had come out on top in the end.

"Nice win," Raoul said next to him. "For a moment there, I thought he was done. Going against a taller, stronger rival…"

Nicolas smiled. "Ah, but in *savate*, speed and precision beats pure brawn. If you rely too much on brute strength, you simply exhaust yourself and your reflexes slow."

"Well, that would explain why I've seen you beat men twice your size, skinny as you are."

"I'll show you skinny, you great ox," he replied with a laugh. "Care for a match?"

In truth, he might come out victorious so long as his burly, dark-haired friend didn't enter the ring with his knife, but just barely. Raoul Prevost had one of the deadliest blades in all of Paris, and his reflexes were as quick as they were lethal.

"I don't fight for sport," Raoul growled.

"Yes, you simply let others do it and place a wager on them."

"But I always bet for your men, don't I? You should be thanking me."

Yes, and today, Boutin was going home with the prize money, of which Nicolas would get a cut. This was a small venue, nothing more than an abandoned warehouse off the side of the Palais Royal where gentlemen came to taste of the more disreputable pleasures of Paris. Working ladies waited for them outside, ready to lead them to the cafés and gambling halls of the area, and finagle them out of the money they'd just won.

A familiar, almost comforting atmosphere, but Nicolas had bigger plans for the men he trained. A real venue, with stands and proper lighting, a betting booth, and most importantly a gymnasium. *Savate* might have been born on the streets, but it deserved its proper place in the sporting pantheon.

It would take more than money, however, for his vision to come true.

Just as he finished congratulating Boutin and collected his money, Raoul elbowed him sharply. Nicolas turned, and the flash of a golden pin caught his eye. A stocky gentleman with stringy hair under his silk top hat shuffled up to him, flanked by a large man with a scarred face. Nicolas crossed his arms in front of him.

"Malenfant," he greeted him. "I thought I saw you lurking in the back, though that pin of yours is anything but discreet."

Two crossed swords, both as long and thick as Nicolas's thumb, shining on the lapel of Malenfant's coat for all to see. A sign that he was utterly unafraid of whoever might have the notion to attack him and steal the pin.

"I do enjoy betting, though I hardly have the need for more money," he replied in a nonchalant tone. "Your man did good. I'm not surprised, given your own skill. I could use someone like you to teach the louts under my command to make better use of their fists. And to knock some sense into those who refuse to cooperate."

Nicolas narrowed his eyes. Raoul sidled closer to him, one hand in his pocket. "What do you want, Malenfant? Coming here with your adjutant?" He addressed the scarred man. "Never took you for a betting kind, Talloche."

"The only thing I'd be willing to bet on here is your head," Talloche said with a gravelly laugh. "Wonder how long you'll manage to hold on to it without protection."

Nicolas sighed. Of course. There were no neutral territories in the capital's underworld. And everyone had to stand on one side or the other. Well, he planned on holding out for as long as he could, no matter how many times Malenfant came to pester him.

"I've already told you, I'm not interested in becoming one of your thugs."

Malenfant's mouth twisted into a sneer. "So you've said. Yet you still owe me a favor."

Indeed, there was that small problem to deal with. His friend Jerome Saint Yves and his wife Stella had come under grievous threat a few months prior, and without Malenfant's help, the whole affair would have ended in tragedy.

"Let's get it over with, then. Have you come to collect?"

"I have no urgent need at the present. Unless you're offering?"

What could he possibly have to offer Malenfant that could

whittle at the colossal debt he owed him? The answer came to his mind with startling clarity.

"Now that you mention it, I might have some information you'd be interested in. Three nights ago, I was at the Opéra Comique and I caught a pair of cutpurses at work, but I believe they weren't under Chardon's orders. Chardon works for you, does he not?"

Malenfant's gaze lit with keen interest. "He does. But how can you be sure they weren't some of our people? Do you know every pickpocket in Paris by name?"

Nicolas raised an eyebrow. "You'd be surprised. Just a hunch, that's all."

Let me go. Please.

The young woman's pale eyes rose to the surface of his memory. As they had many, many times since he'd seen her. Along with her voice. And the feeling of her lithe body against his as he held her captive.

"I could find out, if you like," he offered. "Get you their names. See if your enemy has ordered them to move on your territory, perhaps find out his next move."

Malenfant considered his offer for a moment, stroking his golden pin with his thumb. "Very well. I'll see what that information is worth once I have it. Good day, gentlemen."

He touched the tip of his hat and strolled away with Talloche. Around them, the venue had emptied, and there was almost no one left but a boy spreading sand over the bloody ring.

Raoul took his hand out of his pocket. "Devil take that pompous ass. And now he's got you running errands for him."

"An errand *I* suggested," Nicolas remarked. "I am indebted to the man, loathe as I am to be reminded of it, and I have to admit those two pickpockets tickled my curiosity. The woman in particular… She struck me as odd."

"Odd?" Raoul smirked. "Are you sure that's the word you're looking for? I should have known you had an ulterior motive."

"Don't I always?" Nicolas nodded toward the door. "Come, I

think I know where to start fishing for information."

"Why should I go on this wild goose chase with you?"

"Because," he replied with a pointed look, "we're going to find Suzanne, and she'll be much more amenable to helping if you're the one doing the asking."

Raoul made a sound halfway between a grunt and a groan. "Fine. But you're buying me a drink afterward."

Chapter Three

THE COLD, CLEAR air sharpened the glow of the lights lining Vivienne street. The windows of the cafés and cabarets gleamed like molten gold, inviting passersby to escape the wintry chill for the price of a few drinks.

Nicolas pushed through the door of the Cabaret Doré with Raoul following close behind. The scent of sweat and liquor hit him like a punch to the throat. In a corner, a girl was singing in a raspy voice to the raucous cheers of some of the patrons. Young men, most of them, students and workers, filling their stomachs with cheap wine when they didn't have enough for a proper dinner. Nicolas had been in their position all too often in the past.

"Look, there she is," Raoul grumbled.

Nicolas turned. Short hair the color of cognac, a heart-shaped face dotted with freckles, a satin rose pinned to the low bodice of her dark gray dress, Suzanne Foucher stood behind the counter, wiping a glass with a rag. When she spotted Nicolas and Raoul, her lips stretched into a grin.

"Dear Suzanne, the prettiest flower in Palais Royal." Nicolas took her hand to kiss it.

Suzanne raised an eyebrow. "Nicolas Lefevre, ever the sweet talker. But I prefer the strong silent type. They're far less trouble." She turned to Raoul, and her smile widened. "I'm so glad to see you. You haven't come in a week! I was starting to wonder if I should simply drop by your barbershop and see if you'd taken ill, or worse."

His eyes darted sideways to avoid her gaze. "We've been busy," he muttered. "Big *savate* fight tonight."

Suzanne leaned forward, her low neckline revealing creamy freckled skin and plump curves pushed up by her stays. Nicolas bit back a laugh. If Raoul wanted to look elsewhere, she wasn't going to make it easy for him. "So what can I get you?"

"Two glasses of chartreuse," Nicolas said. "And a very small favor."

Suzanne's smile vanished, and she planted her hand on her hip. "What is it this time?"

"We're looking for someone."

"Of course, you are, damn you," she replied with a snort. "Does that someone owe you money, or is it the other way around? In any case, I don't see how—"

"Neither, as a matter of fact," Raoul interrupted her. "It's a woman."

Her eyes narrowed. "A lover?"

Raoul scratched the back of his neck. "No, she's a pickpocket."

"She could be both," Suzanne replied in a softer tone, and gazed up at him from beneath her eyelashes. "Nimble hands can come in useful for all sorts of things. I should know, I picked my share of pockets back in the day."

"Precisely," Nicolas intervened. Raoul's face was taking on an alarming shade of red. "You see, this woman we're looking for was working in Chardon's territory."

"Under his orders?"

"That's the thing. I'm not sure. She looked like... a lady."

Suzanne laughed. "A lady, and not a lowly wench such as I am, you mean?"

Raoul glowered at her. "Don't say that. That's not what he meant."

"True, my dear, I would never call you that," Nicolas replied with a smile. "My God, if you're lowly, what does that make me? But this woman seemed out of place. And if she was working where she shouldn't be, that could mean someone is knowingly disregarding territory lines."

No need to elaborate. Suzanne knew the unspoken borders of the underworld as well as he did, and the cardinal rule that stated no one should cross them unless they were looking for trouble. "So you need Chardon to confirm or deny your suspicions," she said. "Maybe even give you a name."

"You've known him for years. If you could ask him…"

Suzanne shook her head. "Not a chance. He'll just try to lure me back into his bed."

"You were involved with Chardon?" Raoul asked sharply.

She waved her hand and took a bottle of chartreuse from the shelf behind her. "Ages ago. We had some laughs, nothing serious. He wasn't my protector or anything like that."

Protector. The word always left a bitter taste in Nicolas's mouth. Young men, barely more than boys, would use it to lay claim on a girl in the eyes of their gang and their rivals. But there was usually very little protecting involved, and he himself had learned this the hard way.

Suzanne, though, had never needed a protector. Not when a flock of her cousins worked for Malenfant. At any rate, she was quite capable of defending herself. Nicolas had once seen her bite a man's hand until she drew blood because he'd grabbed her bottom.

She poured their drinks in one swift movement. "Anyway, I could certainly use my charms to coax information out of that fool, but I'm a respectable woman now."

Nicolas held up his palms. "Heaven forbid. Though if Chardon gets the wrong idea, I have no doubt you'll put him in his place. Can't you simply ask him and see how he reacts?"

She slid the glasses over to them, a mischievous glint in her brown eyes. "I suppose I *could*, if someone made it worth my while."

Nicolas slapped four coins onto the counter. "I'm nothing if not generous with my friends, and I'm glad to count you among them."

She took them, put two in the till and slipped the other two into her pocket. "Indeed. But a girl needs more than money to warm her heart on a cold winter's night. Heartfelt words are rarer and more precious than gold."

Nicolas nudged Raoul sharply with his elbow. Raoul shot him a dark glare. Good Lord, what was the man's problem? Suzanne was lovely, vivacious and made no secret that she was sweet on him. Yet Raoul seemed to fear her more than a thug armed to the teeth.

He turned toward her and cleared his throat. "Well, I... We'd be most grateful if you could help us. That said..." He hesitated for a moment before continuing. "Whatever you do, don't put yourself in harm's way for our sake. I'll ask Chardon myself if I have to."

Suzanne's cheeks grew pink, and she sighed. "Oh my, how could I possibly say no to that? I'll get you what you need. Now drink up and tell me more about this mysterious lady."

THE MAID WAS pinning the last flower in Violette's hair when the door burst open. She jumped in her seat. Blast, couldn't her brother knock for once?

"Who the bloody hell is this?"

Emile was leaning against the door frame and glaring at the maid. Violette glanced at her reflection in her handheld mirror and nodded.

"That will be all," she told the girl. "You may go now."

"Thank you, *mademoiselle*," she replied, her voice barely above a whisper, before scuttling off like a mouse.

Emile's bloodshot gaze followed her all the way out of the room, then he turned back to Violette. "You didn't answer me."

"Because the answer is obvious enough to anyone with his wits about him," she shot back. "Just a maid Lenoir sent to help me get ready for tonight."

She rose from her chair and smoothed the burnt copper silk of her dress. A beautiful gown, she had to admit, though the ruched bodice dipped lower than she would have liked.

"Damn it, Violette," Emile snarled. "Every time I step out of my room, there are strangers out and about in my own home. Am I expected to abide such a thing?"

Lord, she was tempted to smash the mirror against the wall. No, better. Over his head. "*Our* home," she replied through gritted teeth. "No thanks to you. You would have seen us thrown out into the streets with your drinking and gambling debts if I hadn't stepped in."

He shook his head. "The same old tune. Everything's my fault, is it? If you'd managed to marry that wealthy old codger, we wouldn't be in this predicament."

Right. Because the De la Roque name still carried its weight in certain circles, namely aging aristocrats whose sole intent was to re-establish their bloodlines after the Revolution had depleted their family trees. Shortly before his death, her godfather had tried and failed to make a match for her with a baron missing half his teeth. The man had already buried two previous wives. Admittedly, Violette hadn't been particularly amiable the only time she'd met him, as it had taken all her energy to hide her outright disgust at the thought of marrying him.

Violette sighed wearily. "It's pointless to argue. The only thing we can do is try to get ourselves out of this situation."

She wasn't naive enough to believe the work she was doing would one day reimburse the totality of Emile's debts to the Boneman. She had no way to keep track of how much the goods she stole were actually worth. But she sometimes kept a few coins for herself with the vague, distant hope that someday, she might raise enough to leave.

Where would she go? What would she do? There was nothing and no one waiting for her. Starting a new life elsewhere was simply a foolish dream.

Emile nodded slowly, his brow furrowed, and for a moment, she caught a glimpse of the boy he'd once been. Shy and serious, often lost in thought. The memory pinched at her heart. It seemed like a century ago.

"You're right, sister," he finally said. "As it happens, I'm meeting a friend later. He said he might have a job opportunity for me."

She frowned. "Meeting him where?"

"At the café. So if you could give me a few francs…"

A cold laugh burst from her lips. So that was why he'd come to her room. She should have known, for most of the time he cared nothing of her whereabouts. "Do you take me for a fool? I'm not giving you money so you can drink yourself into a stupor again."

Though he would find other ways to get the bottle he so desperately craved. His brow was sweaty, and his hands trembling slightly. God help her, nothing she could do would keep him away from that poison.

Emile wrinkled his nose in disgust. "Acting all high and mighty. Didn't Lenoir give you that tawdry gown?"

"Yes, because I can't very well wear a threadbare dress to a *salon* where most women will be dripping in jewelry." She slid on her shawl over her shoulders and took her reticule from her bed. "Now *please*, if you could simply stay out of—"

"You're nothing more than his whore," Emile spat. "He's taking you to fancy *salons* now, but how long before he pimps you out on the streets?"

Three strides, and her hand met his cheek with a resounding crack.

"If you keep at it, brother, you'll be cold in the ground before he does," she hissed. "Have a pleasant evening."

She hurried out of the apartment and down the stairs, slipping on her gloves as she went. Even wrapped tightly in her shawl, the wintry air bit at her skin, and she was glad to see that Lenoir's fiacre was already waiting for her.

When she stepped inside, Lenoir greeted her with a courteous smile. It was the first time she'd seen him in tailored evening clothes. The effect was disturbing. Her eyes saw an elegant, good-looking man, his evening jacket following the lines of his muscular figure, his hair neatly coiffed and his jaw clean-shaven over a white cravat. But her heart and mind knew what lay behind the illusion.

"You look ravishing, Violette," he said. "The girl did a good job with your hair. Do you like your dress? Here, unwind your shawl so I can see how well the color and cut suit you."

Her stomach roiled with discomfort but she loosened the hold on her shawl. "It's… perfectly suitable for our mission."

"Mission?" Lenoir repeated with a little laugh. "Why, this is a pleasant evening out on the town. As a matter of fact, the jollier we are, the better. Remember why we're attending Girard's salon in the first place."

Violette nodded. No picking pockets tonight. "I fail to see why you needed me, if you're simply trying to secure an invitation to Monsieur Girard's next house party."

His gaze drifted from her face to her bosom and back. "A man with a beautiful mistress is less likely to draw suspicion and far likelier to draw interest."

She curled her hands around the edge of the seat. How long would it take for Lenoir to demand that she do more than playact the part of his mistress?

But far worse than Lenoir's intentions was her own uncertainty. Would she resist, or simply give in out of desperation?

No. She *wouldn't*. Or else that would prove Emile right.

"Now then, put a smile on those pretty lips," Lenoir said. "I insist you enjoy yourself this evening."

Chapter Four

NICOLAS'S BOOTS HIT the pavement and he strolled up from the fiacre to the townhouse, a three-story building with tall windows and stucco friezes of twisting vines. One didn't hurry when one was a *bourgeois*, no matter how bloody freezing it was. And tonight, he was no longer a hardened *savate* trainer of Palais Royal, but a gentleman of leisure wearing a dark velvet coat, breeches the color of crushed raspberries and a bronze damask waistcoat. The ability to blend in with any layer of society was an even more useful skill than fighting or wielding a knife.

He paused at the door. If Suzanne's information was correct, he'd have to find a way to thank her properly. She'd come to Saint Aphrodise yesterday morning, wrapped almost to her freckled nose in a gray wool shawl. Nicolas had been practicing with two of his pupils in the middle of the abandoned church that served as his gymnasium. The ring was little more than rope and what wood was left of the broken pews.

"I have what you asked of me," she'd announced triumphantly, her words echoing in the stony nave.

As he'd ducked between the ropes to greet her, she'd glanced around the empty chapel. Disappointed that Raoul wasn't there, obviously, but she said nothing and simply smiled at Nicolas.

He'd kissed her cheek, still cold and rosy from her walk. "You are an angel. I take it Chardon was amenable to your request?"

"Ha! I didn't even have to go to him." She'd lowered her voice to a murmur. "My friend Nanette is dallying with a tall chap they call Bravard. When she got wind of me wanting to know who was picking pockets at the Opéra Comique, she came to me. You see, Bravard works for the Boneman and he got paired up with a lady—*your* lady. Nanette is the jealous type, she doesn't like that one bit, so she wasn't too worried about exposing her."

"*Sacredieu*, someone should write a play about this."

"Anyway, her name is Violette de la Roque. Fancy, just like you said. But there's more. I know where she'll be tomorrow night."

One hundred and twenty-seven Bonne Nouvelle Boulevard. Anatole Girard's house. Nicolas had asked Hortense de Vijeux to secure him an invitation, though she would not be attending the salon herself this week. One of Girard's' friends of her acquaintance had agreed to vouch for Nicolas.

Two birds, one stone. Girard was richer than Croesus, and he was known to invest in all sorts of ventures. Perhaps getting on the man's friendly side could benefit Nicolas in the long run.

Though now that he was here, he hesitated. Gaining entrance to Girard's circle was one thing. Approaching Violette, if she was indeed there, was quite another. Even if he did manage to speak to her, what would he say? Though his mission was to gather information for Malenfant, his burning curiosity was outside the realm of reason or logic.

Violette de la Roque. He repeated the name in his mind, then it rolled off his tongue in a whisper, as if his ears wanted to hear exactly what music it made. *Violette de la Roque.* An *aristo*, then, one whose family had fallen on hard times. No, plummeted and crashed to the ground, more like. Had her relatives been exiled? Or had the Widow taken their lives like it had taken his own father and brother, with one swoop of its blade?

Blood running between the cobblestones…

Nicolas shook the thought away. Not now. He took a deep

breath and rang the bell.

A *majordome* opened. Nicolas gave his name, but he suspected his attire and the silver pin in his cravat were more compelling arguments in his favor. The *majordome* stepped aside to let him in and bright, gilded warmth enveloped him. Girard's house fairly screamed money, heaps and heaps of it, money so new it gleamed in the luster of the mahogany furniture, in the gold plating of the ornaments, in the finely chiseled mirrors that lined the corridor.

How tempting it was, when faced with such splendor, to ignore that misery existed outside. How easy to forget the horrors that had led to this shiny new world emerging from the ashes. At least for one evening. He gave his coat and hat to the footman and smoothed his palms over his waistcoat.

The *majordome* led him to a crowded sitting room. Nicolas entered with a smile on his face. A few of the men looked him over with a practiced air of indifference, but the ladies let their gazes linger a bit longer, fluttering their feathered fans.

He took a glass of wine from a tray, his gaze traveling over rouged faces, bright ribbons and sparkling rhinestones.

"*Monsieur*, I don't believe we've met."

One lady, bolder than the others, sidled up to him, and after a few pleasantries, she took him by the arm to join a conversation about a poetry anthology one of the guests had recently published. Not a subject he cared for much, but then he couldn't very well attend a salon and remain tongue-tied like a timid schoolboy.

"I think it's commendable to explore other verses than alexandrines," he replied when pressed for his opinion on free verse. "We are creatures who seek variety, in the arts or otherwise."

"Well said, *monsieur*," one of the gentlemen agreed. "Take our host, for example. He changed mistresses twice in the last three months, though I will say in his defense that they were all blonde."

Laughter echoed around Nicolas, but he was no longer listening. He'd caught sight of a tall, slim silhouette in a dress the color of freshly polished copper. The woman had her back to him, but something about her long neck and light brown hair…

She turned her head to the side. *Her.* A fine nose, sharp cheekbones, strong brows… Unmistakably her, though Bravard was not by her side.

God bless Suzanne and her chatty friend. Perhaps he should wrap a bow around Raoul and have him delivered to her door.

He excused himself and made his way through the throng of guests. She stood on the side of the sitting room, glass in hand, unsmiling. When she spotted him, her eyes widened with recognition, then darted from side to side. Her hand tightened around the stem of her glass. A frightened cat but a cornered one. Better watch out for potential claws.

He greeted her with a nod. "Mademoiselle de la Roque. So glad to see you again."

She swallowed visibly, but held his gaze, her pale eyes aflame with anger. "Only a cad would use a lady's name without being properly introduced," she replied, every word dripping with icy disdain.

"You're right, how unforgivably rude of me. Nicolas Lefevre, at your service, *mademoiselle.*"

She lifted her chin and straightened her shoulders. Whatever her present circumstances, she still held herself like a gentlewoman, though her dress was far from what a sheltered young lady might wear. The burnished silk shimmered in the candlelight, and the low neckline tempted his gaze to slide down her neck and look his fill. Yet he kept it firmly fixed on her face. No use infuriating her any further.

"Well, Monsieur Lefevre, have you come to finish what you started at the opera?"

He smiled. "That depends. Have you come to resume your activities?"

"If I have," she replied in a low voice, "your only concern should be to walk away before that silver pin in your cravat disappears."

By God, he couldn't remember the last time a woman had

spoken to him this way, if ever. Defiantly. Contemptuously. And his blood was all the more heated for it. Was it simply annoyance? Or something else?

"If I were you, I would not test my reflexes," he murmured. "As it happens, you piqued my curiosity. There's something about you and your presence at the Opéra Comique that doesn't add up, and I'd like to know first and foremost who you're working for."

"Is that so? Well, who are *you* working for, *monsieur*?"

He leaned in closer and his nose caught a hint of lavender soap. "Perhaps I came here of my own accord."

Her lips parted but she stumbled for an answer. "I... I find that hard to believe."

"Really? On the contrary, I find it exceedingly easy to believe." His gaze flitted to her lips. "Can you not think of a reason why I would seek you out?"

"Back away if you know what's good for you," a man growled behind him.

Nicolas froze. He knew who that voice belonged to. And every time he heard it, it brought unwelcome echoes of the past.

He turned and faced Jacques Lenoir, who was scowling as if he'd just stepped in horseshit. Nicolas couldn't blame him, as the feeling was entirely mutual. Ten years ago, they had roamed the streets together, drank and fought and whored in the same gang of streetwise thugs. Back then, Nicolas thought of Lenoir like a brother. Now, he was more like a malevolent shadow, hellbent on reminding Nicolas of who he had once been.

And if Lenoir was involved with Violette, it wouldn't the first time Nicolas saw him treating a woman like his personal property.

He sighed wearily. "So we meet again. Damn it all, Lenoir, when am I ever going to be rid of you?"

"I could ask you the same thing." Lenoir side-stepped him to grab Violette's wrist. "Now what were you doing talking to my special friend?"

VIOLETTE'S HEART THUDDED painfully fast as she looked from Lenoir to Nicolas Lefevre. They were glaring at each other, one burly and dark, the other lean and golden. Lenoir's fingers dug into her skin, a warning to stay silent, but he needn't bother. She couldn't speak. She could scarcely draw breath.

Lord, they looked like they were about to jump at each other's throats. And if they didn't, Lefevre might reveal what happened at the opera the other night. What if Lenoir, or worse, the Boneman chastised her for being careless and drawing an enemy's attention?

"Your special friend." Lefevre's green eyes blazed, though his expression remained cool. "Did your master bid you put your mistress on his payroll, or did you come up with that idea on your own? I wouldn't be surprised either way."

Mistress. Violette wanted to pull away, to scream a denial. An hour earlier, she had not flinched at the implication when Lenoir had introduced her to their host. But hearing the word aloud hit her like a punch to the gut. It was as if she had crossed the line from playacting to reality.

"I will not discuss this with you here," Lenoir snapped, and he glanced around to see who might be listening.

Lefevre raised his eyebrows. "Would you rather come by Saint Aphrodise to have a little chat between two *savate* lessons? Perhaps we might discuss it in the ring." He rolled his shoulders back and Violette was suddenly reminded of how effortlessly he'd kept her in his strong grip. "By all means, let us not be indecorous in such company. We wouldn't want anyone to find out just how ill-bred we are. Except, I gather, for Mademoiselle de la Roque, who is just the opposite."

He met Violette's gaze. His lips seemed to be fighting a smile. Who on earth was this man that he could smile in such a situation? He utterly confounded her. He had discovered her name. Learned where she would be tonight. And now it seemed as if he was trying to be… friendly, almost.

Lenoir's fingers dug deeper into her wrist, and she winced. Lefevre's expression hardened, like a flame blown out by a gust of icy wind.

"You ought to be careful how you a treat a lady," he said, his voice cold and unyielding as flint.

A movement fluttered on the edge of her vision. His hand flexed, tightening it into a fist.

Lord almighty, this had to stop before a fight broke out. "Please, *monsieur*, I do not need your assistance."

Lenoir tugged on her arm possessively. "Do not trouble yourself, Violette. We shall leave at once."

Without giving Lefevre another look, he pulled her across the room and through the crowd toward the corridor. Violette glanced back to find a pair of emerald eyes watching her, unflinching, but Lenoir quickened his steps and she hurried after him amid the whirl of colorful gowns and curious stares. After waiting for their coat and shawl in stony silence, Lenoir dragged her out into the freezing darkness.

"Let go of me," Violette demanded. "You're hurting me. Surely, you can trust me to follow you now that we're in the street."

"Shut your mouth," he barked, his tone coarse and rough.

He didn't speak again until they were aboard their fiacre and jostling down Bonne Nouvelle Boulevard. "How does Lefevre know you? Tell the truth, or you'll wish you'd never spoken to that whoreson."

Panic seized her throat. A better question was how on earth Lenoir knew *him*. The animosity between them had not sprung up from this encounter alone. She forced her voice to remain steady. "He spotted me and Bravard at the opera. Nothing more."

Lenoir clenched his jaw. "Nothing?"

She nodded, eyes wide. Hoping to appease him. Hating that she must, when she really wanted to scratch his eyes out and bolt from the fiacre. "Before tonight I did not even know his name, nor did I tell him mine. He discovered it on his own."

"That fucking bastard has always been too nosy for his own good," Lenoir snarled. "If he thinks he can meddle with our affairs... No, the master will know how to deal with him. I must inform him right away."

"Right away?"

This time, there was no keeping the waver out of her voice.

Lenoir stared out the window as the wide boulevard gave way to a narrow, winding street. "The sooner the better. And you're coming with me."

Chapter Five

A CACOPHONY OF shouts, cheers, and drunken debates hit Violette like a wave the moment she crossed the threshold of Café Baladin with Lenoir. From the outside, fogged windows masked the typical Latin Quarter crowd. Yet here and there, scowling men with scars hunched over, heads together, in hushed conversation.

They were always here, even when Violette met Lenoir during the day. The Boneman's escort, no doubt hiding arms beneath their cloaks and ready to strike if an enemy dared set foot on their territory.

Violette lowered her eyes. Several of the men greeted Lenoir, and their gazes crept over her, sending shivers over her skin.

Jaw clenched, Lenoir led her all the way to the back of the café. A guard with a bent nose stood with his arms crossed at the foot of a flight of stairs, but he let Lenoir and Violette pass without a word.

Her knees threatened to give way with each step she climbed. She'd only been allowed upstairs once, after a couple of thugs had beaten Emile black and blue. It could have been so much worse. They hadn't broken any bones, but the message was clear. *Pay up or else.*

Violette had come to plead on his behalf—not for mercy, for

there was none to be found in this godforsaken city, but for work. It was the only time she'd met the Boneman, until now. Her heart clawed its way up her throat. *Don't panic. Breathe. Let Lenoir speak.* Acting like a frightened mouse caught in a trap would only make things worse.

Upstairs, a corridor led to a line of doors, some left ajar. In the various rooms, men in silk waistcoats and shirt sleeves played billiards or roulette under the watchful eye of scantily clad women with painted lips. Behind the closed doors, high-pitched cries left no doubt as to what other activities were in the offing.

A ball of dread weighed down her stomach. If the Boneman gave free rein to Lenoir to claim her…

Don't panic. One foot in front of the other. Again. Again. No use despairing over something that had not yet come to pass.

At the end of the corridor, two more henchmen flanked a double door.

"I need to talk to Estienne," Lenoir said.

Estienne? The Boneman had a name then, though she had never heard Lenoir refer to him as such.

"Master doesn't want to be disturbed," one of the henchmen grumbled.

"Go tell him it's about Lefevre."

The man grunted, knocked four times, slowly, and entered the room. A minute later, the door opened. Lenoir yanked Violette inside.

The room matched her memory with its burgundy wallpaper and sparse furnishings. A chest of drawers, a side door, and a large, sprawling desk strewn with letters, envelopes and a massive, leather-bound ledger.

Black, stringy hair flopping into his face, the Boneman, scribbled a letter. His quill continued its scratching while they waited. Finally, he signed his name with a flourish and looked up.

A shudder traveled along Violette's spine. Light brown eyes, narrow and keen and filled with cold, calculating intelligence, honed in on her like a bird of prey on the lookout for a kill. They lay in sunken sockets, in a deathly pale face.

Did they call him the Boneman because he was so gaunt? Or for some other, more sinister reason, like the rumors she'd heard? She hoped to God she would never find out.

"You've come with news of our old friend?" His soft, cultivated tone stood out in stark contrast to his surroundings.

Our old friend. The Boneman knew Nicolas Lefevre too, then. Fate was cruel indeed to have this man, of all people, catch her in the act of picking a pocket.

"He tracked us down tonight," Lenoir replied. "Showed up at Anatole Girard's place. He was looking for *her* after spotting her at the opera."

He nodded toward Violette. The Boneman's gaze flickered over her but he kept his attention focused on Lenoir, as if she was nothing more than another piece of furniture.

"Are you sure he wasn't looking for you?"

Lenoir opened his mouth but struggled to get the words out. "I... I am quite sure, yes."

"This isn't the first time you've crossed paths with him lately," the Boneman pointed out, his gaze sharpening. "Nor is it the first time you've let him chase you away without completing your mission."

"He's been a thorn in my side—in *our* side—for years now. We should simply—"

"Kill him?" The Boneman tapped his long, thin fingers on the desk. "His skills would be valuable to us. If it came down to it, I'd sooner kill you. Perhaps I should make him that offer. Your head against his allegiance. Do you suppose he might accept?"

Lenoir swallowed audibly. "Lefevre won't be turned."

"He's put up a good fight so far, I'll admit. But every man has a weakness. One must simply find out what it is."

The Boneman smiled, the skin stretching over large, perfectly aligned teeth. The smile of a blood-thirsty beast. He dug into a drawer and produced a small pouch. He placed it on the desk, coins tinkling inside.

Then he turned to Violette. "Tell me, my dear, has Lenoir acted in a courteous manner toward you, like I asked him?"

She nodded, though her blood turned to ice in her veins. "He has, *monsieur*."

"Good. No putting his hands where he shouldn't? Or trying to peek under those pretty skirts?"

A hot flush burned her cheeks. Lord, let this be over soon. Let her return home. Let her be spared this humiliation. "No, *monsieur*."

"Good. He has always been an obedient dog." He leaned back in his chair. "Lenoir, strike her."

Her eyes widened. Surely, he couldn't…

The slap stung her cheek before she could even finish her thought. She pressed her cold palm against the throbbing and glared at Lenoir who stared back blankly. Damn him. Damn him to hell. If the Boneman wanted his head, at that moment, she'd be more than willing to do the job herself.

"Strike her again."

This time, Violette braced herself. She raised an arm and ducked, so Lenoir's fist hit the side of her head. The blow was still strong enough to send a pulse of pain through her skull. She pushed him back furiously, and he growled like a beast, grasping her wrist to twist her arm.

The Boneman watched them with what looked almost like glee, his grin widening. "Down, boy. Mustn't leave too many bruises. She's worth more to me unsullied." Lenoir released her, and the Boneman tossed the pouch of coins to him. "Here's your treat."

Lenoir shoved the pouch into his pocket. The Boneman was right, he was nothing but a dog. A dog who would beat her, rape her, put her to work on the streets the moment his master snapped his fingers.

"What am I supposed to do about Lefevre, then?"

"You'll do nothing for now," the Boneman replied flatly. "He and Malenfant's men took down the Kingfisher and his smugglers not six months ago, and Malenfant has been trying to get him to join his ranks ever since. If Lefevre wants to bed this girl and you go looking for a fight, you'll drive him straight into that whoreson's arms. Just do as you're told."

Lenoir scowled but pressed his lips together and said nothing. The Boneman picked up his quill and started writing again without sparing them another glance. Lenoir took Violette's arm, and she followed him out.

"You heard him," he growled next to her ear when they were in the corridor. "Tomorrow you go back to work with Bravard. And you had better come back with your reticule full to bursting if you know what's good for you."

"Why, will you beat me bloody?" she shot back before she could stop herself. "Or will you ask your master for permission first?"

He halted in the middle of the corridor and pulled her brusquely to him, eyes dancing with wild fire. "Mark my word, you little bitch, the longer I hold out, the worse it'll be for you. Now get out of my sight."

He released her and hurried off to one of the gambling rooms, leaving her to hurry down the stairs alone, nearly tripping at each step in her haste.

Her mind raced as she made her way out of the café, her heart pounding and an iron fist squeezing her lungs. She was running out of time. Either Lenoir would snap, or the Boneman would finally decide that she had more value as a whore than a pickpocket. She needed to find a way out, and fast.

What about Emile? They would kill him if she ran, and then they would still catch her. Without money or connections, she would not get far from Paris. But if she stayed, she was the one who would end up dead. Or broken beyond repair.

Out in the street, she closed her eyes and forced several deep breaths in, as if the cold air could cleanse her. When she opened her eyes again, tears blurred her vision. She could trust no one, no friend she could turn to.

She wiped her tears before they could spill. Devil take it, she didn't need a friend. She needed muscle. And for that, the enemy of her enemy would do just fine.

"IF I WERE you, I would just forget about her."

Nicolas stared at the ceiling. Raoul's blade ran over his jaw fast and fluid as water, cold against his skin. Nicolas waited until the blade lifted before replying. "What on earth are you talking about?"

Raoul uncorked a small bottle and the scent of bergamot tickled Nicolas's nose.

"Don't take me for a fool." Raoul slapped the cologne on Nicolas's cheeks. "You've had that *look* on your face all day."

Nicolas ran his hands over his jaw. Smooth as silk. Not only was Raoul the only man in Paris he trusted with his shave, but he never left the slightest bit of stubble. "What look?"

"Like your mind isn't all there. Before you know it, you'll be tripping over your feet and taking punches from your own pupils."

Nicolas snorted. "That's rich, coming from the man who barely lets out more than a grunt when Suzanne is around."

Raoul unpinned the towel draped over Nicolas's chest and tossed it onto the table next to his blade. "I'm not going to let any woman get under my skin and muddle my thoughts, and you should do the same. You have more important things to worry about right now. Forget her."

Blast. Maybe he shouldn't have told Raoul about the previous evening at Anatole Girard's house, but then if Lenoir was involved, he really had no choice. That meant the Boneman already knew Nicolas was on Violette's trail, and that was certainly something they should all be worried about.

He didn't fear Marcel Estienne. He'd known him far too long

for that. An image of a scrawny, dark-haired boy flashed through his mind. A boy who made up for his slight frame with twice the toughness and three times the cruelty as the other orphans roaming the streets. Setting fire to a woman's hair in a tavern and clapping as she gesticulated to put it out. Picking a stray cat off the pavement and slicing its throat with a giggle.

Estienne had always thrived on chaos, and Nicolas had no intention of letting that chaos threaten the life he'd built. That scrape with the Kingfisher while coming to Jerome's aid had been close enough. But now…

"The Boneman is becoming too bold," he said. "Overconfident. He's sending people like Violette de la Roque to work on Malenfant's territory, and he's got half the *gendarmes* in the city on his payroll."

"Then let Malenfant deal with it. Give him the information you gathered and move on. You told me you didn't want to get involved."

Nicolas rubbed his freshly trimmed nape. Indeed, he didn't. Over the years, he'd amassed a small fortune in the gambling halls of the Palais Royal, first playing, then working for the owners to make sure patrons didn't win too much or too often. But *savate* matches, he found, were a far more thrilling venture, and just as lucrative. The thud of flesh meeting flesh, the sweat, the fury coming off the fighters and the roar of the audience… It made his head spin like liquor. Next to it, the roulette table seemed as bland as watered-down beer.

Besides, he enjoyed training pupils in the art, teaching them how to defend themselves, making them understand the value of discipline. A man who could make proper use of his fists and feet wouldn't find himself helpless in the face of adversity. A feeling Nicolas didn't wish on anyone.

But if he wanted to build a career out of it, he couldn't afford to get mixed up with either Malenfant or the Boneman.

Forget Violette. A different vision emerged on the surface of his memory. Pale, blazing eyes and a creamy neck. The smell of lavender… He shook his head. Even if he did forget her, how long could he remain neutral?

"You're right," he finally said. "Malenfant is already breathing down my neck as it is."

Raoul cleaned his blade with a rag, folded it, and put it back in his pocket. "Not to mention that any investor you find for your gymnasium could very well be a friend of his. The Boneman may have *gendarmes* on his payroll, but Malenfant rubs shoulders with men in high places."

Nicolas sighed and stood from the chair, eager to change the subject. "Come now, let us go have dinner. We won't solve anything on an empty stomach."

They didn't pursue the matter. They had work to do that evening anyway, as a royalist group had hired Raoul to store their printing press and bundles of newspapers in the back room of his barber shop, a job best done at night.

Yet after Nicolas returned to his suite of rented rooms just above the southern gallery of the Palais Royal, his thoughts circled back to Violette and Lenoir.

He took off his jacket, setting it on the upholstered chaise next to his bed, then unbuttoned his waistcoat. Damn it all, could Violette really be Lenoir's mistress? She did not give the impression of a well-pleasured woman. Quite the opposite, in fact.

Stiff. Tense. Flinching ever so slightly when Lenoir touched her. Voice lined with ice, despite the fire in her gaze.

Had Lenoir forced his attentions on her? His insides clenched. Whatever the case, she was in danger. Nicolas sat on the edge of his bed and squeezed his eyes shut, struggling to keep the memory at bay. It had been lurking since last evening, ready to remind him of the horror he'd witnessed.

Golden curls, a shy smile, always at Lenoir's arm… And Lenoir was quick to warn the other boys that she belonged to him.

I'll punch out the teeth of anyone who touches her. Laurine is mine, understood?

And yet the brute had barely hesitated before handing her

over to Estienne. She'd begged and cried and fallen to her knees. The rope had dug in Nicolas's wrists, pain shooting up his arm, and her screams echoed in his ears...

He stood and walked over to the shelf where he kept a decanter of cognac on a silver tray. He poured himself a glass. The cognac heated his throat and chest but left it hollow. He tilted his head back and swallowed the rest in long, greedy gulps. Just enough to blunt the sharpness of his memories, numb the more cutting edges. He undressed and went to bed.

Slumber came and went like a tide, sending him sinking into oblivion for what seemed like a second before retreating again at the slightest sound. Broken glass. A shout in the night. A peal of feminine laughter ringing out in the gallery below.

It was still dark when he left his bed. He hadn't rested properly, but no matter. He needed to walk, to fight, to punch a straw bag over and over again until he was utterly drained.

Outside, the freezing air both soothed and spurred him into a lope. The streets were deserted save for a few rag-pickers and dustmen, and for once Nicolas welcomed the solitude.

What about Violette? Is she alone now? Helpless in the face of adversity, just like you once were?

He shoved the thought away. She was not his concern. Tracking Violette down had been a mistake. One of the basic principles of *savate* was calculating when you could afford to let your guard down to place a lethal kick. But now was not that time. Right now, he would do well to stay in his corner.

Chapter Six

VIOLETTE KEPT HER gaze riveted on the muddy hem of her dress. One shuffling step after the next on wet pavement that threatened to turn to ice at any moment. At the narrow street that led toward the Palais Royal, she stopped and peered at the steps of Saint Aphrodise. Still there. Both of them. Two young men she'd spotted earlier, deep in conversation, wreathed in pipe smoke.

Blast. Should she come back tomorrow? Take one more turn around the neighboring streets to give them another chance to leave? She adjusted her shawl over her hair and kept walking. For two days, she'd observed the early morning comings and goings around Saint Aphrodise. Yet she still hadn't worked out the best way to approach Nicolas Lefevre.

Saint Aphrodise.

Lefevre had mentioned the place to Lenoir, and the name stuck in her mind. Like Aphrodite, the goddess of love, though the run-down stone chapel squatting in a cramped square between rows of ramshackle houses hardly conjured images of grand myths and ancient tales of love.

What had he said about the place? Something about *savate.* She assumed it was some sort of fighting sport, since she'd heard Bravard mention a bet he'd placed on a street match with Lenoir.

Perhaps Saint Aphrodise was an illicit ring.

If so, good. That meant Lefevre was exactly the sort of man she needed to help her. Yet as she dodged the vendors and passersby in the winding alleyways to make her way back to the chapel, a knot seemed to form in her gut. What if Lefevre said no? What if Lenoir somehow got wind of her doings? What if this risk was all for nothing?

You have no choice. She pulled her shawl tighter. Even if Lefevre did refuse, at least she'd have tried. At least Lenoir didn't keep her on a leash, like his master did with him.

The steps of the chapel were empty this time. She approached slowly, letting her gaze travel up to the tympanum. No saints looking down at her, either to encourage her or pass judgment. Their heads had all been hacked off.

She slipped between the half-open oak doors. Shouts and grunts echoed off the cavernous walls. The nave had been cleared of pews, leaving room for a ring of wooden planks and ropes. Surrounded by a group of onlookers, two men circled each other. Despite the cold and damp, sweat glistened on their bare chests in the faint daylight filtering through the broken windows. They hopped from one foot to the other, hands curled into fists, muscles tense. Ready to strike.

"Go on, then! Now!"

Him. Lefevre paced next to the ring, arms crossed, his gaze entirely focused on the fight.

Smack, smack, smack.

One of the combatants lashed out with a series of quick jabs. His foot followed in a vicious kick aimed at his opponent's breastbone. Before the blow could land, the other snaked out a hand to grab his leg. A whirling motion threw the first man off balance. He landed on the ground with a loud thud.

Lefevre leaned over the ropes. "See, you hesitated a second too long. If you're not quick enough, your opponent has time to anticipate you. Right then. Who's next?"

He glanced around, and his gaze landed on Violette. Her

heart thudded painfully, but she returned his stare. His green eyes narrowed.

"Boutin, you spot them," he said. "I'll be right back."

Lefevre strolled toward her, casually, as if he was greeting an acquaintance on a walk in the park. His shirtsleeves were rolled up to reveal corded forearms, and his open collar revealed the notch at the base of his neck. Good Lord, how could he not be cold? His bare skin must be fairly burning. She curled her fingers into a fist against an urge to test her theory.

He nodded courteously, though his gaze was sharp and hard. "Mademoiselle de la Roque. I can't say I was expecting you. Have you lost your way?"

"Monsieur Lefevre." She lifted her chin slightly. "I need to talk to you. Please. It is a rather… urgent matter."

"Given the company you keep, I guessed as much." He studied her for a moment, as if gauging her intent. "Follow me, then."

She trailed after him across the nave, the wordless stares of the others weighing on her shoulders. Lefevre might be teaching these men to fight, but his authority seemed to extend beyond the ring. Her resolution faltered. Did they respect him, or fear him?

He led her to the apse, past where the altar must once have been and through a door to a small room. The vestry, now filled with sacks of straw and a pile of rope. Violette loosened her shawl to uncover her hair.

"I know you do not have much time," she said, "so permit me to be direct."

He held up his palm. "Before you do, I must ask you something, just so my conscience is clear. Has Lenoir sent you?"

She blinked. "No. No, of course not."

"*Of course not.*" He repeated the words with a little laugh. "It's a natural assumption, I assure you. The first thing anyone from this world would think. But then, you are not from this world, are you?"

Her cheeks heated under his piercing gaze, but she would not look away. "Lenoir doesn't know I'm here. In fact, I would rather not contemplate what he would do if he found out."

The corner of his mouth lifted. "Fear not, your secret is safe with me. If you've come to me, you must have guessed that Jacques Lenoir and his master are no friends of mine."

She nodded. "Indeed. And I have no one else to turn to for help."

He raised an eyebrow. "What sort of help? I should tell you right away, as much as I detest them, I'm not an assassin for hire. Though you would not be the first to make that sort of request."

A shiver ran over her skin. Under his suave words and nonchalant manner, how dangerous was this man?

"No, I need…" She hesitated. "I need to learn how to defend myself. How to fight. It appears to me others are here for the same purpose."

For several long moments, he said nothing, then took a deep breath as if to calm himself. His eyes lingered on the reddish bruise on her temple. "Has Lenoir harmed you?"

She bit her lower lip. "He struck me, at the Boneman's behest."

Lefevre raised his fingers as if to touch her, then clasped his hands behind his back. "I see. Nothing else?"

A different kind of burn crept up her neck, and she shook her head. "He did not… Beyond that one time, he is under strict orders not to touch me."

He sighed wearily. "Yes, that's the sort of game that amuses Estienne. He gets far more pleasure from it than gambling or whoring."

"But I don't know how long it'll last," she continued. "And I cannot wait helplessly for the Boneman to decide to let Lenoir do as he pleases. It is… unbearable."

Something gleamed in his eyes. Something akin to sadness, though she could not imagine why. "I understand your predicament. However, I cannot give you an answer straightaway. I must think on it."

She pushed back a wave of disappointment. This was the best

she could have expected. He had no reason to trust her, and no reason to take this risk himself.

"Of course. But I must know quickly if I need to find another solution. If you agree, though, we shall then discuss how I might pay—"

"I have no need for money, or anything you could give me," he interrupted, his tone suddenly harsh. "Do not mention it again. Simply tell me where I can reach you."

"Thirty-one Bergère Street." She retied her shawl. "Pray do not take too long. My safety depends on it."

⇶⫷

NICOLAS TURNED A small glass of green liquor between his thumb and forefinger for a moment before lifting it to his lips. The chartreuse left a familiar, comforting trail of warmth in his throat, but instead of relaxing his mind, it only muddled his thoughts further. Or maybe there was nothing that could help him in this situation.

"Easy, there," Raoul grumbled in the seat next to him. "I won't carry you home if you get foxed."

Nicolas ignored him and called to Suzanne at the other end of the counter. She finished pouring drinks to other clients before sashaying over to them.

"You're certainly thirsty tonight," she said as she tipped the bottle to refill his glass. "That *demoiselle* has you tied up in knots, doesn't she? She must be a bold woman indeed if she came to ask you for lessons."

Nicolas glared at Raoul. "You told her? Damn it all, *now* you decide to loosen your tongue around her?"

Raoul shrugged and stared into his pint. "It's not my fault. I was waiting for you all of ten minutes and she started pestering me. Had you found Violette? What were you going to do about her? A nightmare."

Nicolas shook his head. "I hope you're proud of yourself, Suzanne. You've broken the man."

Suzanne merely laughed. "Hardly. I believe he was just waiting for a chance to ask for another perspective. Really, it's not that complicated."

"I fail to see how," Raoul defended himself. "If Nicolas helps the girl, the Boneman will take it as a declaration of war. If he doesn't…"

"Because you think that scrawny bastard isn't going to go after him anyway? Ha! Nicolas makes himself a target simply by breathing the same air as he does."

"No, Raoul has a point," Nicolas said. "I can't afford to get involved too closely in the Boneman's affairs. Being indebted to Malenfant is trouble enough."

She crossed her arms and leaned on the counter. "You took down the Kingfisher, didn't you? To help your friends?"

"That was different. Stella Saint Yves's life was in danger. If we'd left her in the hands of that heartless scoundrel…"

Suzanne raised an eyebrow. "A heartless scoundrel, you say? A lady in danger? You're right, that is completely different from Violette de la Roque's predicament."

A smile fought its way to his lips. Point to Suzanne. He took another swig.

"I still think provoking the Boneman isn't a good idea," Raoul insisted. "Especially for a girl you've only met three times."

"Oh, you great big handsome brute," Suzanne said with a sigh. "Quick as lightning with a blade, but slower than a lame horse when it comes to matters involving the gentler sex."

Raoul turned his focus back to his beer and drank in long slow gulps instead of answering. Nicolas had to laugh. "Haven't you tormented him enough for one evening?"

Her mouth curled in a cheeky grin. "I'm simply saying that three times might be enough. Or even one time."

Blast, he should stop the chartreuse now, because whatever Suzanne was implying was too close to what his gut was telling him. That one look at Violette was all it had taken to pique his curiosity. And talking to her alone that morning, in the closed spaces of the vestry, had awoken another type of curiosity. One that urged him to stroke her face and test how soft her skin was, to unwrap her shawl and let down her silky curls.

That curiosity, he had to keep it under tight control. He'd be damned before he gave Violette the impression that she might repay his services in kind.

"Believe me, I have no other intention than to lend Violette my assistance," he finally said.

Suzanne's grin softened into a gentle smile. "I believe you, Nicolas. I know why you want to help her."

Yes. Suzanne would know, and so would Raoul. He'd told them both on separate occasions what Estienne had done to Lenoir's girl, all those years ago. And how they had forced Nicolas to watch.

I protect her and she lets me bed her. If you ask me, she's getting the better end of the deal.

That was the way things were done in the streets. Nothing out of the ordinary, and yet it has always left a bitter taste in Nicolas's mouth. But the bitterness had swallowed him whole after that hellish night, and he'd nearly drowned in it.

He pushed his empty glass away. *No more. Keep your wits about you. You're going to need them.*

Raoul frowned. "Well, as long as you're training Violette, you might as well give Malenfant what he wants. The more information you obtain, the more of your debt you'll be paying back."

Nicolas snorted. "Ah, so *now* you think it's not such a bad idea after all?"

Raoul downed his pint. "Around here, you have to learn to make the best of terrible situations."

Chapter Seven

VIOLETTE DRAGGED HER aching feet to the door of her building. An evening of dancing with gentlemen under a sparkling chandelier, wearing a silk gown, in the grand room of an *hôtel particulier*. For Young Violette, this enchanted vision would have been a dream. Now such an event was only a night of work with Bravard, and a bitter reminder of the illusions she'd lost.

Her younger self could have never imagined the lancing pain in her calves, the leering gazes and malodorous breaths of said gentlemen, and especially not having to slip her hand into their pockets to retrieve silver watches and coins.

She was about to cross the threshold when she felt a soft tap on her arm. Her heart leaped in her chest and turned to find a small boy peering up at her. Even in the dim light of the street lanterns, smudges of dirt stood out on his pale face.

"Mam'selle de la Roque," he said, his voice high and musical as a flute. "I've a message for you."

He handed her a folded note, and she frowned. "At this hour? How long have you been waiting here in the cold?"

"Not so long. My master told me you'd be out until late."

She could only hope the master in question was Nicolas Lefevre. Then, at least she could pick pockets knowing she was not utterly defenseless. She unfolded the note to find sparse but elegant writing.

Tomorrow at noon, twenty-nine Caumartin street. –NL

Her pulse quickened. He had accepted, then.

She thanked the boy and fished into her reticule for a coin, but he simply shook his head and grinned.

"M'sieur Lefevre told me not to accept anything. He pays me in hot meals and *savate* lessons, so it's well worth my while."

She raised her eyebrows. "*Savate* lessons? At your age?"

"M'sieur Lefevre says it's never too early to learn."

Or too late, God willing. "Would you happen to know where twenty-nine Caumartin street is?"

"North of the Palais Royal, past Capucines Boulevard. Number twenty-nine is the brothel with the mermaid, you can't miss it." He touched the brim of his shapeless wool hat. "Evening, *mam'selle.*"

She watched him dart off into the shadows. A *brothel?* Lefevre wanted her to meet him at a *brothel?* She shook her head and pushed through the door. She shouldn't be surprised. He was a street-hardened scoundrel, same as the rest of them, despite his courteous manners. Even his charm was a mask, nothing more.

She hurried up the steps. *You can still change your mind. You don't have to go.* True, she could find another way.

But as soon as she entered her home, her misgivings vanished. The flat was dim and deserted. No domestic waiting up, no embers burning on the hearth, not even the familiar sound of the soft, rhythmic breathing of loved ones deep in sleep. Just the frozen moonlight casting shadows from the windows. Shards of broken glass glistened on the floor of the dining room, and the door to Emile's room was wide open, revealing an empty bed.

He had disappeared again. Lord knew when or in what state he'd return. Her brother might think the same of her when he watched her leave in the evening. That is, if his mind weren't constantly clouded with liquor.

No, she could not continue in this manner. This wasn't a life; this was barely survival. Unwrapping her shawl to undress and slip on her nightrail, then wrapping it around herself just as quickly to burrow under a moth-eaten blanket and threadbare sheets. Closing her eyes and praying for sleep to take her quickly. Not knowing what miseries tomorrow might bring.

Enough. Tomorrow, she'd meet Lefevre. This was what she wanted, what she counted on to improve her lot, however small or futile a change it might make in the end. Better a brothel in his company than the most elegant of parties with Lenoir. Or ending up at the brothel herself, when the Boneman saw fit to place her there.

THE NEXT MORNING, Violette set off with her determination intact, though an uneasy feeling roiled in her stomach. When she'd risen that morning, Emile's bed was still empty, and indeed she had slept through the night undisturbed.

Lord, what if he was lying cold and dead in a gutter somewhere? How long before she should go looking for him?

She crossed Capucines Boulevard, lifting her hem and sidestepping piles of horse dung. *He has disappeared for longer periods before.* Four days, to be exact, and not long after they had settled in Paris. Their uncle had searched for him in vain, before Emile had staggered into the flat one morning, deathly pale, with a gash on his cheek.

Back then, she still believed he could change, that her care and attentiveness could shield him from these evil temptations. Now she could only hope he kept living and breathing one more day.

Do not think of this now. She glanced up at the street signs and located Caumartin Street. Moments later, she stopped in front of a large mermaid, painted on a wooden facade, under the words

La Sirène.

"Excuse me, might you be Nicolas's friend?"

A young woman in a plain wool dress scurried up to her, eyes alight with sharp curiosity. Her short reddish-brown hair, upturned nose and freckles gave her an almost childish appearance, inviting trust rather than suspicion.

"I am," Violette replied. "He told me to meet him here."

The young woman smiled. "Pleasure to meet you, *mademoiselle*. I'm Suzanne Foucher."

It seemed absurd to introduce herself using her full name. Whatever precedence she might have had once had died long ago. "Please, call me Violette."

"Come along," Suzanne said. "Nicolas is inside. He thought it might be safer if no one saw you together in the street and asked me to wait for you out here. No one will pay a *grisette* like me any mind."

Was Suzanne Lefevre's mistress? Wouldn't that make her a target as well? Perhaps she was simply someone else he paid to run errands for him, then. Violette followed her in. Blast, she could not possibly ask, but the question nagged at her for some reason.

The entrance of the brothel was painted in shades of dark blue and turquoise, decorated with a fresco of seashells. A few had fallen off here and there, leaving gaps.

A stout woman lumbered into the entrance, hair disheveled, wearing a lurid green dressing gown that gaped in the front. "How long is this nonsense going to take?" she asked Suzanne in a gruff voice. "We open at two."

"Don't you worry, Lili, you won't even hear us leave," Suzanne replied.

The woman grunted, glanced at Violette with bored indifference, and turned to leave. Suzanne sighed and led Violette down a flight of stairs.

"Lili is my cousin," she explained. "Or my half-sister, we're not quite sure. She's a Foucher in any case, and a real cow, but she did agree to let us use the ballroom in exchange for a few francs."

"The ballroom?"

The stairs were so narrow both her elbows nearly brushed against bare brick. How could anyone possibly imagine a ballroom here?

But then the stairs opened into a wide area with a low ceiling, carved into the rock underneath the building. Mirrors on the walls gave the illusion of space, though most were pitted and dulled with age, and they reflected the light of candelabras.

Lefevre paced in the middle of the room, arms crossed over his chest. When Violette reached the bottom of the staircase, he stopped and pivoted on his heel. His lips curled into an easy smile.

She held his gaze for a moment before looking away. His lack of jacket reminded her of the last time she'd seen him. She had an idea now of what lay beneath those linen shirtsleeves—strong forearms dusted with golden hair—but at least the collar was buttoned. Thank goodness. She could cling to some notion of propriety, though an inkling of something else curled in the back of her mind. The same ticklish feeling she'd gotten when she wondered just how hot his skin was to the touch.

He nodded. "Pleasure, as always. I hope you find this place acceptable. No chance of anyone spotting us here."

Violette unwrapped her shawl. "Indeed. I admit I was surprised that you would suggest a brothel, but then I didn't expect you to invite me to your regular training sessions."

"With all those louts? I wouldn't dream of it." His smile grew teasing, almost rakish. "Saint Aphrodise is no place for a lady."

She raised her eyebrows. "Do you mean to suggest this is?"

He stretched out his arms. "Of course. It's a ballroom. Don't you agree, Suzanne?"

Suzanne laughed. "You're asking the wrong person. I know nothing about what befits a lady." She turned to Violette. "However, I could give you a few tips when it comes to defending yourself. Probably more useful than whatever fancy footwork this fool is going to teach you."

Violette smiled. She was starting to like this woman. "I'd be delighted."

Lefevre made a flicking motion with his hand, though his eyes glimmered with amusement. "That's quite enough, now. Go and stand guard and let me get on with it."

Suzanne stuck out her tongue but did as he asked. No, she couldn't possibly be his mistress. The way they teased each other…

Violette's heart lurched painfully. Just like her and Emile, so long ago. Brother and sister.

"Are you ready?" Lefevre asked.

Violette swallowed the bitter taste in her mouth and let her shawl drop. "Yes, *monsieur*. Let us begin."

Chapter Eight

"THE FIRST RULE if I'm to train you is you must stop calling me *monsieur*."

Nicolas planted his fists on his hips and straightened his shoulders, the stance he assumed to hand out lessons to his *savate* students. No matter if they were bigger than he was, adopting a posture of authority always persuaded them to listen more than the rules of politeness dictated. That and beating them soundly in the ring if they questioned his skill.

Though he was almost a head taller than Violette, for some reason, he needed to assert his position. Perhaps because none of his previous students had eyes quite so mesmerizing. Or lips so soft and delicate as rose petals. Or tantalizing curves that plain gray wool didn't manage to hide. *Get a hold of yourself, man.*

"In the ring, we only use our given names," he continued. "I may be the teacher, but if my students call me *monsieur*, they won't want to punch me as badly."

Violette frowned. "I'm supposed to want to punch you?"

He grinned. "Believe me, you'll soon be dying to do it."

Spots of red bloomed on her cheeks. Easy to fluster, this one. Much too easy for his own good.

"What shall I call you, then?" she asked.

"Nicolas. Or Lefevre, whichever you prefer."

"Nicolas." The three syllables rolled off her tongue like music. "Will you call me Violette, then?"

She was already Violette in his mind. Not *mademoiselle*. Not her fancy *aristo* surname. Just Violette, with her beautiful eyes and lavender scent.

"Or De la Roque, if you'd like," he replied. "It's a good fighting name. Tough. Spectators like that."

Her lips stretched into a small smile of contained amusement, but it reached her gaze in a gentle glimmer. Something seized in his chest. For a moment, the mask of worry and suspicion had lifted, giving him a glimpse of youthful, luminous charm.

Good Lord if life had not been so cruel to this woman... He shook the thought away. They all had to play the hands dealt to them. And this was precisely what he was here for.

"Violette is fine," she said. "I don't think I'll be fighting in the ring any time soon."

Nicolas unbuttoned the top of his collar. "Well, you'd have to get rid of those skirts, for one."

The flush returned to her cheeks and spread to her creamy neck. God help him, he couldn't help but wonder if other parts of her body would take on a similar hue in more pleasant circumstances. *Tell her that, and she might just scratch your face off before you even start.*

He cleared his throat. "For now, a basic exercise will do." He grabbed her shoulders to position her directly in front of him, at arm's length. Devil take it, as appetizing as her womanly curves were, her shoulders were nothing but skin and bones. When was the last time she'd eaten properly? "Make fists and plant your feet solidly on the ground. Then try to touch me."

She raised an eyebrow. "You mean punch you?"

"No. Touch me." His words came out raspy. "You have to learn to walk before you can run."

Her eyes blazed at his challenge, and she curled her fingers. She aimed for his gut. He blocked her hand effortlessly and shoved it back. She pressed her lips together and tried again. Her fist landed smack in the center of his palm. Again, and again, in quick succession. Deflecting her efforts was as easy as batting away a shuttlecock.

Too easy. Her gaze betrayed her intention every time, and she moved too slowly. She increased her pace, but only managed to narrow her range. She snarled through her teeth at every dull thump of her fists.

Finally, she dropped her hands. "Blast."

"Catch your breath and try again. But this time, don't look where you're aiming."

"I have to," she said. "I need to aim properly."

"No. For now, you only need to touch me, and I'm a rather large target, wouldn't you say?"

She ran her gaze over him, up and down, before averting it again. "Indeed."

"Besides, it should be easy for you. You already know how to move your hands without watching, or else you wouldn't be much of a pickpocket."

She turned her nose up at him. "That's not the same thing."

"How is it different?"

"Stealing requires stealth. Discretion." From the corner of his eye, he caught her hands curling back into fists. "Growing up, I was taught to be seen and not heard, to speak only when spoken to, to walk in a soft and ladylike manner. I... I started stealing small objects just to see how quiet and unnoticeable I could be. Or even if I could disappear altogether. It gave me a strange sense of satisfaction. So when I offered my services to the Boneman to repay my brother's debts..."

Her brother? The information prickled his curiosity, but also inflamed his anger. What kind of wastrel would leave his own sister in the hands of a monster like Estienne?

"Was it drink, then? Gambling? Women? Or any combination of the three."

Her eyes hardened. "Drink. Emile should never have come here. He wasn't ready for it, not when we were orphaned and already struggling to get by. Paris ate him alive."

Her tone was almost accusing, as if he had something to do with it. Or maybe she simply resented the fact that some people were better equipped to survive life in this formidable chaos of a city.

"Believe me, I understand more than you know. But I can see why the Boneman put you to work picking pockets. Your talent is undeniable."

Or else Estienne would have found another use for her. The flame of fury spread within like wildfire. Why had Violette been spared so far? Surely such a beauty could earn more entertaining wealthy clients than she would picking pockets. Unless Estienne was negotiating with several interested parties and trying to drive up the price—auctioning off her virginity if such was the case.

He could not bear to tell her. Could not bear to even think of it. But he couldn't remain silent, either.

"The debt will never be repaid," he said quietly. "You know that, don't you?"

Violette nodded, her eyes filled with sorrow. "If I leave my brother to his fate, they'll kill him. Emile is a coward and a drunk, but he's the only family I have left. And I have nowhere else to go."

His own brother's face rose to the surface of his mind. *Leonard*. The years had robbed Nicolas of the memory of Leo's voice, but some images were as vivid as ever. The quick work of his hands when he kneaded dough. The blazing fires of the bread oven casting a glow on his ruddy face and blond hair. His booming laugh—so similar to their father's.

Would he have sacrificed himself to save Leo if he could have? Or his father? A pointless question. The Revolutionary Tribunal was more ruthless that the Boneman and Malenfant put together, and the Widow never missed her mark.

But Leo had been a good man. A brave man, right up until the end. From what Violette was telling Nicolas, the same could not be said for Emile.

No, he must find a way to get her out. Preferably without everyone involved ending up in Montparnasse Cemetery.

Walk before you learn to run. Training first, then scheming.

"All right," he said. "Try again. And if you don't want to be tempted to look…"

He took a scarf from his pocket. Her eyes widened. Was she going to back down now? But almost immediately, her gaze hardened again.

"Fine. Whatever you think is best."

TAP. TAP. THUMP.

On her fourth try, her knuckles landed in the brocade cloth of Nicolas's waistcoat, the fabric soft against her skin. A warm sense of accomplishment filled her. At last. It had taken three lessons in the basement of the brothel, but she'd done it.

With any luck, she could do it again. And again.

"Good. Very good. Turn around."

Nicolas worked to untie the knot at the back of her skull. "You see now, don't you? *Savate* isn't about brute strength. If it were, you would not stand a chance against Lenoir or any other of the Boneman's thugs. Speed and deception. Count on those. Make your enemy underestimate you. Lead him to expect one move and then—"

She whirled, arm outstretched, and almost hit his flank, but Nicolas's fingers curled around her wrists, stilling her hands. By God, he was quick. Quicker than she'd imagined. And the pressure of his fingertips on the delicate skin of her inner wrists…

Almost gentle, yet his underlying strength buzzed through every nerve ending. Made her crave a different sort of touch, one she had never experienced before, an idea that glimmered darkly but remained shrouded in mystery, out of reach. She pulled out of his grasp and batted at the locks of hair that had fallen from her chignon.

His gaze followed the movement of her hands. "Well done. You almost had me there."

There it was again, growing stronger. A feeling she couldn't name bloomed in her chest and tugged deep in her body. Pride? There was pride in it, something she thought she'd forgotten. Pride mixed with something. Something new and daunting.

"Now you're ready to learn where to aim," Nicolas continued, and pointed to a spot in the center of his chest. "Put your hand here."

She drew closer and placed her palm on his breastbone. Heavens, the heat of his skin radiated through his shirt. Burning, like she thought it would be. And the warmth coiled up her arm, gliding over her own skin. She sucked in a breath.

She met his gaze. His eyes burned even more, like emerald flames that pierced straight through her.

"Press harder," he murmured. "Do you feel that hollow just between the ribs?"

She shook her head. His solid muscles felt like rock under her touch.

"*Harder.*"

She pushed with all her might. Finally, she felt it. A slight indent between the bones and the hard knots of muscle. She snatched her hand back. Her head was spinning, her limbs heavy. Water. She needed water.

"There are three places you must aim for with hard, purposeful blows," he continued. "This spot on the chest with a solid forward punch. Then the nose, upwards with the base of your palm." The corner of his mouth lifted. "The third will require a kick."

Violette smiled. "A kick, or a knee? I imagine Suzanne could teach me that one. Though I was wondering if you were planning on teaching me how to use my legs and feet."

"Certainly. Go ahead and kick me right now."

Without warning, she whipped her toe upward. Before she could make contact with his shin, his hand wrapped around her knee, grip tightening to hold her in place. Her other leg wobbled. A steadying arm prevented her fall.

"You're not steady enough yet." His voice was low and thick, as if he too was struggling to keep his thoughts clear. "It's all about balance."

"Balance," she repeated blankly, for it was impossible to form a sentence with his hand holding her knee and the other splayed on the small of her back and *oh*…

He released her leg abruptly. "Hands first, then feet. But by all means, go ask Suzanne for a trick or two."

Violette rolled her shoulders and straightened her back. "Perhaps it might help me if I came to see a real *savate* match. That way I could see how your other students apply your techniques. Or how *you* fight."

"You wish to go to a match surrounded by blood-thirsty, screaming louts?" He laughed. "Forgive me for thinking that isn't a very sound plan."

"Why not? If you were there…"

She would feel safe. As if his very presence might ward off those who wished to harm her. *Foolish girl. This isn't a fairy tale, and he's no prince.*

Still, her curiosity prodded at her, conjured images of Nicolas in the ring, facing a rival as quick and ruthless as he was. What would it be like to see him in action, feet dancing, arms jabbing and slashing through his rival's defenses? Sweat gleaming on his skin…

"*Savate* matches take place at night, in any case." Nicolas smoothed his waist coat with his palms. "Impractical."

"At Saint Aphrodise, then."

He sighed. "We'll see. Come then, that's enough for today."

His expression closed off. No use insisting, but he had not deterred her. On the contrary. Their daily meetings had lit a flame in her like a bellows fanning embers to life. She managed to conceal it, to keep it burning low when she wasn't with him. Emile had finally returned, but he slept through the morning and had not even noticed her absence, and Lenoir had seemed satisfied with the pickings of her last two outings.

Find a way. Heed your desire. Now that she'd tasted victory, however small, she wanted more.

"Go on," she told Nicolas. "I'm staying a bit. Could you send Suzanne down here?"

He nodded. "At your service."

Moments later, Suzanne sauntered down to the ballroom with a smile. "Nicolas told me you needed my help with something."

"Two things, actually. Though the second one you'll have to keep to yourself. It's a bit... bold."

Suzanne's smile widened to a grin. "Bold, you say? I know a thing or two about that."

Chapter Nine

"**P**LEASURE, AS ALWAYS."

Nicolas slipped his wool coat over his massive shoulders. While she watched him dress, something tugged at Violette's heart. A deep, lingering ache that could only be lessened with the word *tomorrow*.

"Yes, I'll see you tomorrow."

Three days ago, she'd shared her plan with Suzanne, three days of training with Nicolas in the dimly lit underground ballroom, three mornings of strange, undefinable giddiness bubbling up in her stomach when she was on her way to meet him, followed by a long, agonizing wait that stretched through the afternoon and evening, driving her to distraction.

Last night, she'd almost gotten caught picking the pocket of a gentleman during a lights display in front of the Tuileries. An easy mark. Everyone was enraptured by the strings of colored lanterns lighting the square, but she'd pulled the purse too hastily and the gentleman had turned around, forcing her and Bravard to make a run for it.

Careless. Foolish. It could not happen again. If it did, getting caught by the *gendarmes* would be the least of her worries.

Nicolas buttoned his coat. "Before I go, there's something I must tell you."

Her heart gave a little jolt and her mind started to race. Was he about to say they couldn't meet any longer? Inevitably, there would come a point where there would be no *tomorrow* left, but... *Not now. Just a little while longer.*

"I'm listening," she said cautiously.

"If you're to train properly, you must eat well."

She blinked at him. She certainly hadn't been expecting *that.* "I beg your pardon?"

"You can't fight properly on an empty stomach." His expression had hardened into concern. "Are you getting enough to eat?"

She stared down at her feet. "We manage."

It wasn't an outright lie. She and Emile weren't starving, after all. They did manage, though she couldn't remember the last time she had felt satiated, or truly enjoyed a meal. But she couldn't bear the humiliation of admitting that to Nicolas.

"Believe me, I know what it's like," he said quietly. "There is no shame in it. I've had to beg for food or steal it more than once in my life. If you are in need of anything..."

"I'm not."

Her words came out sharp. Sharper than she intended. By God, he was only offering to help her, so why was she reacting this way? A strange sort of fear niggled at her. If she came to depend on Nicolas's kindness too much, and he disappeared from her life...

"Thank you," she added in a softer tone, "but the only thing I need is to know how to defend myself."

Nicolas nodded. "Of course. Keep yourself safe, then. Until tomorrow."

Violette waited a few minutes before wrapping herself in her shawl and heading to the entrance of the brothel, where Suzanne was chatting with her surly cousin-or-half-sister near the seashell fresco. The moment Violette reached the last stair, Suzanne scampered up with a grin and slipped her arm into hers.

"Oh good, you're ready to go! I'll see you later, Lili," she called over her shoulder, then led Violette into the street.

Violette squinted against the pale sunlight. "You were waiting for me?"

"Of course. We've got a *savate* match to attend."

"Oh! Right now?" True, she'd asked Suzanne for help in finding out when and where she could see Nicolas fight, but she'd expected more plotting and planning.

Suzanne pulled her with each brisk step toward the Palais Royal. Would she return in time to get ready for the evening? Would Emile notice if she wasn't there when he woke up in the afternoon? No, nothing could penetrate the fog of his mind these days. When Violette had suggested they attend the Christmas service together like they did in the past, he'd merely turned a bleak gaze toward her and asked if she had a few francs on her.

But what about the maid Lenoir employed to clean their home, wasn't she supposed to come today? Even if her brother didn't take note of her absence, the maid certainly would.

"Trust me, this is an opportunity we can't miss," Suzanne replied. "First I thought we might sneak into Saint Aphrodise in the morning so you could watch Nicolas train his students, but then Raoul told me…"

"Who's Raoul?"

Suzanne sighed and batted her eyelashes so theatrically that Violette bit back a laugh. "A dark handsome brute of a man who holds my heart in his palm. And one of Nicolas's closest companions. They met in Marseille when Nicolas fled Paris years ago, then they returned together."

Marseille? How had Nicolas ended up on the other side of the country? And what could have possibly chased him away from Paris? He seemed… fearless. Utterly unafraid of the Boneman and his ilk. Capable of defending himself against the worst sorts of thugs. The string of questions whirled in her mind, begging to be let out, but Suzanne still hadn't explained where they were going.

They stepped onto Capucine Boulevard and bundled together as a cold dry wind swept over them.

"According to Raoul," Suzanne went on, "an investor has

taken interest in Nicolas's *savate* school. They've organized a small tournament at Saint Aphrodise this afternoon, at the man's request."

Violette raised an eyebrow. "Does this Raoul have a loose tongue?"

Suzanne's eyes glinted with impish amusement. "Not by half, but I'm getting rather good at loosening it. The trick is to show him he doesn't intimidate you, no matter that he's a big, brawny fellow who can slit a man's throat as if it were made of butter. He might make your knees weak but you're woman enough to handle him."

"I see." Violette had never heard anyone talk about seduction this way. Suzanne made it sound almost easy. "And that works, then? You and Raoul…"

"Not yet. For once I'm trying to get *him* to do the actual wooing, and that's much trickier than simply luring a man to your bed."

"You seem to know quite a lot about the topic." Suzanne frowned, and a flush of embarrassment stung Violette's cold cheeks. "Forgive me, I did not mean to cause offense. On this subject, I am utterly ignorant, and I would not even know where to start if… Well, if I wanted to…"

Suzanne watched her from the corner of her eye. "And is that the case?"

Violette stared down at her feet. "No, of course not."

It couldn't be the case. Could it? For as long as she had known what took place in a marital chamber, the idea of laying with a man had filled her with disgust. When she'd turned fifteen, her mother had explained to her the necessity of preserving herself for her husband and had described in vague terms what her wifely duty would entail—lying in bed and keeping absolutely still while some unpleasant, often painful coming and going took place between her legs.

Illness had already taken hold of Maman, and perhaps she had sensed she would not live to see Violette married. But then

Violette's uncle had tried to find a match for her and the feeling of dread had only rooted itself deeper. Now it gripped her throat every time she was in Lenoir's presence.

With Nicolas, however... When his brilliant green gaze settled on her, when he caught her hand or leaned closer to correct her position, the disgust melted like ice before a fire into nothing more than an unpleasant memory. That mysterious nameless feeling took its place, hot and dizzying, gripping not her throat, but deep in her belly and between her legs. Simply thinking about his rakish smile, the way his golden hair curled on his forehead, the low, smooth pitch of his voice ignited that liquid sensation.

She bit her lower lip. Lord help her, but she didn't want that feeling to stop.

"Well, if you should ever happen to find yourself in that situation, I'm here to help," Suzanne said lightly. "Your secrets are safe with me."

"That's very kind of you."

Yes, she could trust Suzanne, perhaps more than she could trust herself. She was already taking too many risks. And yet with each step bringing them closer to the Palais Royal, excitement bubbled up within her again, drowning any trace of fearfulness.

"How will we get inside unnoticed?" she asked Suzanne.

Suzanne grinned. "A secret passage. Too small for Nicolas or any of his students, but you should be able to squeeze in."

When they arrived at Saint Aphrodise, Suzanne led her to the side of the church to a small door. It still hung on its hinges, but part of it had been smashed in, leaving a narrow gap between broken planks. Suzanne crouched and wiggled through. Violette followed suit. The splintered wood snagged at her shawl and scraped against the wool of her dress, but she managed to push through.

A rumble of shouts and voices filled Violette's ears, but the wall of a narrow wooden staircase separated them from the sanctuary. She followed Suzanne up the rickety steps, carefully placing her feet so as not to make the ancient wood creak, to a loft overlooking the church. Had an organ once stood there? If so, there was no trace left on the smooth stone.

"On your hands and knees," Suzanne breathed. "They won't see us that way."

The two of them crawled along the stone balustrade. Violette's pulse quickened as the cold stone bit into her knees and palms. Between the columns, she caught a glimpse of the savate ring. It was empty, but men crowded it on each side, jostling, drinking, calling out names—one in particular, repeated by several. *Boutin! Boutin!*

Suzanne glanced back at Violette with a short nod and sat down, hugging her knees, peeking down at the crowd.

"Best view in the building, wouldn't you say?" she whispered.

Violette smiled. "Indeed. Boutin, is he one of Nicolas's students?"

"Yes. Look, there he is."

A mountain of a man entered the ring along with his adversary—shorter by a head, but hopping nimbly from one foot to the other. Violette scanned the crowd until her gaze landed on a head of curls the color of burnt gold. *Nicolas.* He wasn't at the side of the ring this time, but speaking with a gentleman in a silk hat. Next to him stood a dark-haired man with broad shoulders and a ferocious glower.

"And that's Raoul," Suzanne added, following Violette's gaze. "What I wouldn't give to see him in the ring!"

"He doesn't fight?"

"He does, but not for sport, unfortunately. So I can only hope that one evening he'll get into a quarrel at the cabaret."

A shrill whistle pierced the air and the match started. Boutin slammed a fist dead center into his opponent's gut. The other man barely wavered. His foot lashed out and hit Boutin square in the chest. The smack of flesh on flesh echoed against the stone. Boutin staggered for only a moment. Then with a roar, he grabbed the other man's legs and flipped him over. His back hit the ground with a thud.

Another match, another pair of fighters. And then another. Violette's gaze struggled to follow the fighters' rapid blows. But her attention kept slipping back to Nicolas. His eyes were fixed on the ring, his expression hard and stern. A sharp command would sometimes burst from his lips, but he was no longer talking to the gentleman next to him. Yet as soon as a match ended, his expression would lighten, smooth over, and he would exchange pleasantries with his guest again. As if he was slipping a mask on and off at will.

"Go on, Lefevre," Boutin shouted after the most recent match-up. "Jump in. Or are you afraid to wrinkle those fancy clothes?"

Nicolas laughed, and his fingers found the buttons of his waistcoat. "If that's a challenge, you know I'm always glad to take you on."

"No, me!" a younger man cried out. "It's my turn now!"

Nicolas shook his head. "Not a fair match, Richieux."

Richieux pounded his chest with his fist. "You afraid I'll punch out your teeth, old man? Try me and see!"

Violette frowned. Nicolas's fingers hovered over the buttons, but the crowd clamored for the match, shouting out both their names. Finally, Nicolas shrugged off his waistcoat and untied his cravat. A roar of approval rang out in the nave.

"Oh my, he's really going to do it," Suzanne said. "Richieux hasn't been fighting that long, but he's tough as nails. This could get interesting."

Violette couldn't answer. Her mouth had gone dry at the sight of Nicolas kicking off his shoes and stockings. Then, his fingers curled into the fabric of his shirt, untucking it before pulling it over his head...

She'd felt his firm, unyielding strength under her fingers, but it was nothing compared to witnessing his corded muscles rippling under smooth skin, pale as marble and just as exquisitely defined. Longing rose within her. Her palms itched to run over it, stroke every hard ridge, explore every angle. The very idea robbed her of breath, roused the nameless feeling again right from her core, stronger this time, impossible to contain.

The whistle trilled. The match was starting. She shook her head to clear her thoughts.

Nicolas circled his opponent, his movement lithe, cat-like, calculated. And then he lunged.

Smack. Smack. Thump.

Chest. Face. Kick. Just like he'd told her. But God, it looked so different when he did it. His hands and feet flashed like lightning into a string of lethal blows. And lord help her… it did things. Forbidden things. Flames curled in her midsection, coiled in her veins, threatened to engulf her. She felt each slap of skin on skin deep inside, and her mind reeled with the desire to have that same strength seize and claim her.

Richieux hit back with furious energy, managed to land a punch on Nicolas's brow. Nicolas's head snapped back and droplets of blood splattered the ground. He regained his bearings, a crimson rivulet pouring down the side of his face, and attacked again. His blows were even faster, more precise. Chest. Face. Kick. Kick. Kick.

Richieux reached for Nicolas's thigh and tried to spin him, but just before losing his balance, Nicolas pulled him into a headlock and they tumbled to the ground in a heap.

A sickening crunch. A cry of pain. Then silence.

"No!"

Violette covered her mouth with her hand. Too late. The word slipped out of her mouth and echoed on the stone walls.

Nicolas staggered back up, panting hard, his right arm cradling his ribs. His adversary writhed in pain, but Nicholas wasn't looking at him. He was staring straight in her direction, his green eyes blazing with anger.

Chapter Ten

NICOLAS STARED UP at the loft. Every breath he took sent a fresh wave of pain up his side, but the anger boiling within him was almost enough to make him forget the throb of his bruised rib.

What the hell was Violette thinking, sneaking behind his back? Had she any idea of what could happen if the wrong person saw her here? When would one more risk become one risk too many?

Violette remained frozen in place for a moment, eyes wide, locked with his, until Suzanne stood up next to her and pulled her away. The two women disappeared.

Raoul ducked between the ropes of the ring and crouched next to Richieux, "I'm going to have to take care of this, and fast."

Richieux. Devil take it, he must be in a far worse state than Nicolas was. No mistaking that cracking sound. Indeed, his opponent lay still, breathing hoarsely, his skin pale and covered with a sickly sheen of sweat. His right shin was bent at an odd angle, the bone almost jutting out, though it hadn't broken the skin. Nicolas's stomach lurched. All things considered, a flesh wound would be less unpleasant to look at.

Lesson learned, at least. The poor bastard would think twice before challenging a superior fighter.

He turned toward Raoul. "Can you do it here?"

"I could set the bone, but I don't have anything to make a proper splint. And I'm not too keen on doing it in front of an audience."

Point taken. The other men crowded around the ring craning their necks, jabbering and passing flasks around, almost as if they expected a more thrilling show. Nicolas scanned the area beyond the crowd in search of the gentleman who'd requested the tournament. Guillaume de Marbois stood, eyebrows raised and hands clasped behind his back, betraying nothing more than mild interest.

Nicolas raked his hand through his hair and exhaled. "*Sacredieu.* Do you think we could carry him to your shop with Boutin's help?"

Raoul grunted. "It's only two streets over, and a far better place to work in peace and quiet. You're not carrying him, though. That was a nasty hit you took. I'll have to check to see if your rib's broken."

"Right. Let's go, then."

Between finding the best way to lift and carry Richieux and scattering the crowd, it took a few minutes for them to get going. Boutin and Raoul set off, but Nicolas hung back to bid Marbois good day.

"I'll be in touch, Lefevre," the gentleman replied in a courteous tone, as if they were in an elegant *café* and not a run-down church where a man had shattered his leg in a fight. "This was most entertaining."

Impossible to tell from his sphinxlike expression whether he meant it, or what he was referring to. The fight and the injury? Either way, for an *aristo*, he certainly had solid nerves if he found it *entertaining*.

"At your service, *monsieur*."

Nicolas slipped his jacket over his shirt and unbuttoned waistcoat. Outside, Violette and Suzanne were waiting, wrapped in their shawls.

He met Violette's gaze, and anger bubbled up afresh. Something burned in her eyes, but it wasn't shame or remorse. Quite the opposite, in fact. A strange sort of determination. As if she was telling him without words she'd rather take his chastising now rather than later.

Damn her to hell, this woman was too brazen by half, and now his anger warred with fire of a different kind.

"Will Richieux be all right?" Suzanne asked. "Raoul just told us his leg was broken."

"Raoul will do what he can. We'll see."

Violette took a few steps toward him. "What about you?" she asked, almost softly. "Are you hurt?"

He clenched his jaw. Was she genuinely worried? Trying to appease him? No, she wouldn't get away with this so easily.

"Suzanne, take her the long way to the barbershop," he snapped. "And wait for me there. I have a few things to discuss with her."

→»»»×«««←

"ALL RIGHT, GIVE him a few swigs of that. It ought to calm him."

Nicolas uncorked a bottle of clear liquor. A pungent scent filled the room, and Violette pressed her nails into her palm.

Breathe through your mouth. It'll pass.

This was no time to get sick or, worse, faint. The sight of Richieux's broken shin was enough to make cold sweat run down her back, and the smell of alcohol was making it worse. But Nicolas had insisted she remain within his sights, in the backroom of Raoul's barbershop.

They'd laid Richieux on a large table, where Boutin pinned him down. No chance he'd dash off, but violent tremors wracked his body.

"Don't touch me," he wheezed with the wide-eyed stare of a trapped animal. "Don't touch me. Just leave it. Don't…"

"Unless you want to spend the rest your life walking with a

limp, you'll stay put," Nicolas said. "Go on, drink."

Richieux whimpered, and Nicolas pressed the rim of the bottle to his lips, tipping it so he could swallow. Richieux coughed, and tears sprang from his eyes.

"No more," he begged. "You'll kill me." He glanced at Raoul, who was leaning over the table, inspecting his shin. *"He'll* kill me."

"If Raoul wanted to kill you, believe me, he'd be much quicker about it."

Nicolas tipped the bottle again, once, twice, three times more. Richieux's eyes lost their focus. His words jumbled together in a slur.

"Bloody fucking… barber doesn't know…"

"There, all better." Nicolas nodded at Raoul. "Proceed, doctor."

Violette bit her lip. How could Nicolas be so callous? It was as if the gruesome injury he'd caused left him cold. As if he'd done this hundreds of times before.

You knew he was a dangerous man. She should not be surprised. Why, then, did she not recoil in fear and disgust from him? Her reason, her reserve, her gentle breeding, all of it turned to ash when the fire took hold of her.

Raoul aligned himself with Richieux's legs. "Boutin, keep your grip on his shoulders. Nicolas, you take that wooden brush and put the handle between his teeth so he doesn't chop his own tongue off and make a bloody mess. Right, now hold his wrists. Nobody move or make a sound until I'm done."

Suzanne grasped Violette's hand, and squeezed her eyes shut. "I wouldn't watch if I were you," she whispered. "Trust me, you don't want to see this."

Violette closed her eyes, but the raspy wail that filled the room was enough to freeze her blood. Seconds ticked by, and the wail turned into a drawn-out sob that seemed to go on and on.

"There. Ready for a splint."

Violette opened her eyes again. Richieux's head drooped to

the side. A spurt of vomit burst from his lips.

"Fucking hell," Nicolas muttered. "Better than blood, I suppose."

The smell… It was horridly familiar. Oh Lord, she needed air, or she was going to cast up her accounts as well. She sprang to her feet, but it only made her head spin faster.

Suzanne laid a hand on her back. "Violette, are you all right?"

Air. Outside. *Now.* She ran from the room and burst into the darkened shop, reaching for the door handle.

Strong fingers shackled her arm.

"Let me go!" she cried.

The grip tightened, and pulled her against a solid chest. Him. Her body recognized his presence before her mind, and awareness spread like an eruption of flames where their bodies touched.

"I cannot let you run out into the street in such a state," he murmured next to her ear. "Calm down and tell me what's wrong."

"Everything," she gasped. "Everything inside that room… The smell of alcohol and vomit…"

Emile. It was just like Emile. But if only Nicolas had seemed to care even a little…

"And *you*," she continued, her tone sharper. "You acted as if it was nothing. You broke that man's leg!"

He dropped her arm, and she whipped around. He towered over her, green eyes flashing furiously. "Richieux wanted a fight, I gave him one. Was that not what you came to see, in spite of my reservations? By all means, you should be satisfied."

"I had to take matters into my own hands," she shot back. "How am I to learn *savate* without watching other people fight? I certainly did not think…"

"You did not think a nasty fall and a hard hit could shatter a bone? Tell me, what did you expect? That we would bow politely and pretend to fight like a pair of fencers?"

She opened her mouth, but no sound came out, and a flush rose to her cheeks. No, this was most unlike the posturing dance of a pair of fencers. A fencing match would not ignite a strange, fierce yearning in the very core of her. The way his muscles had rippled with every deadly blow…

He leaned closer. "*Savate* is a violent, dangerous sport. There are rules, of course, but it was born in the streets. You remember that move I taught you, striking your opponent's nose upwards with the base of your palm? You can kill a man that way, if you hit hard enough."

Was he talking from experience? She dared not ask. She dared not move. She could only remain silent and keep her gaze locked with his, for her heart was thudding with such force that the smallest movement might make it career out of control.

"I didn't think it would go this far," she finally said. "You're… different when you teach me."

He laughed. "I would never do anything to hurt you. *That* is the difference."

"I know you wouldn't." The words slipped out before her thoughts caught up with them. But she realized she *did* know. She had known almost from the start. "Else I would not have asked you to help me. It may be foolish of me, but I sensed you were not the same type of man as Lenoir, and you have proven me right."

He stood perfectly still and did not speak for several moments. "When I fell… Did you fear I was injured?"

She nodded. "I was surprised to see you lose your balance. How bad is it?"

He shrugged and lifted the hem of his shirt, revealing a red welt on the ripple of muscles. Her cheeks flushed at the sight. "Just a bruise to the ribs. Raoul looked it over. Nothing broken."

"Does it hurt?" Her words came out in a hoarse murmur.

His Adam's apple bobbed as he swallowed roughly. She wanted to kiss his skin there. Taste it. The hot, pounding rush in her veins was making her light-headed, dizzy. She swayed toward him.

"Violette…"

Her hand slid over his side.

Put a stop to this. Pull back before you are both lost.

She didn't pull back. Couldn't. His gaze pinned her where he stood. His skin was so warm under his shirt, so warm, and she'd been out in the cold for so long…

She rose on her toes, and pressed her lips to his.

They were smooth and plush, slotting perfectly against hers, as if they had been made for kissing her. He raised his hand to cup her face, caress her hair, his thumb stroking her cheekbone. So strong, yet so gentle, and oh, she felt like the inside of her was melting and burning at the same time…

He groaned against her mouth. Was he trying to tell her something? Did he want her to stop? She broke the kiss with a shuddering breath.

"I… Forgive me, I should not…"

He snaked his arm around her waist and pulled her closer. "Yes, you should."

She hesitated only a moment before kissing him again. It was so good, so right that all thoughts and doubts fled from her mind, leaving only the sensation of him, his soft mouth, his hard body against hers.

More. She wanted more.

He nipped at her lower lip, teasing, prodding lightly with his tongue until she let him in with a moan. Oh, this was even better, this was exquisite. She wrapped her arms around his neck, locking them both in a tight embrace, increasing the delicious friction between their bodies.

More, more, more.

His mouth left hers, and she whimpered at the loss, but his lips pressed to her neck now, his breath hot against her skin, and it fanned the flames higher.

"Tell me to stop, Violette," he panted. "*Please.* I'm not strong enough to do it myself."

She arched against him desperately, heeding the relentless urge of her body. "Don't stop," she breathed. "I beg you, kiss me again."

Their mouths met once more, and he slipped his hands to her thighs. Wrapped his fingers around their flesh. Lifted her. Two steps, and he set her down on the wooden counter. Spreading her legs. Pressing a hard bulge right where a throbbing ache built within, swelling, demanding relief. Winding her skirts up and sliding his palm over her stockings.

He *knew*. Knew what she needed, right now, yes, she couldn't wait. She moaned and gripped his forearm, pulled, urging his hand further and further to the edge of her stocking…

"We'll just let him sleep here and—oh, bloody fucking hell."

Raoul. Panic seized her and she pushed Nicolas back, squeezing her eyes shut for a moment before glancing at Raoul, Suzanne and Boutin, who had just come out of the back room.

Suzanne gave Raoul's arm a slap. "I told you not to barge in!"

Nicolas took Violette's hand to help her down but she snatched it back. She couldn't let him touch her again, not when her body was still pulsing with want, begging for relief. What on earth had she been thinking? If they hadn't been interrupted… This was madness. Utter madness, and it had been from the very start.

"I need to leave," she muttered. "*Now.*"

"Wait…"

"Do not follow me, Nicolas."

She turned and fled into the dusk.

Chapter Eleven

ECHOES OF SONGS and laughter drifted to Violette's ears as she peered at the street through her bedroom window. Dusk was still deepening into night, but people were already celebrating the new year. Later, the public squares would host bonfires, musicians, dancing.

She pressed her palm against the cold glass. On the other side lay another world entirely.

What was Nicolas doing this evening? Who would he celebrate with? Merrymaking with Raoul and Suzanne and the denizens of Palais Royal, or sitting at the table of high society hosts in front of a delicious meal? Scallops in cream sauce… Crispy duck and buttery parsnips, served with the finest wine…

She closed her eyes and a different sort of hunger swept through her. Her mind flooded with images of his face, his smile, his muscular arms and strong hands. She could almost feel them on her now, sure and hungry, grasping her waist and sliding up her leg. Feel his lips on her skin, burning a painless brand there that never went away.

Three days. Three days since that moment in the barbershop. Three days of agony, battling with a longing so strong that she nearly trembled with it. She hadn't returned to the brothel. She couldn't face Nicolas and resume their lessons as if nothing had happened.

Lord knew she had tried to grapple with this folly. But Nicolas had awoken a part of her she hadn't even known existed, brought it to life, and now it wouldn't return to its slumber. Worse, it demanded satisfaction, doggedly nagging her whenever she thought of Nicolas, when she lay in bed at night and when she rose in the morning.

Heaven help her, if she found herself alone with him again... Would he refuse her, or give in? Was he more reasonable than she was, or tormented by the same yearning?

"Violette." Her brother's voice called from the dining room. "Violette, there's someone at the door."

"Good God, Emile, can you not answer then?" she huffed as she made her way down the corridor.

"Whoever it is, it's most likely for you, not for me," he muttered.

He was sitting at the table playing solitaire, his hands swift as he slapped the cards down and picked others up. Emile had always been fond of card games, but she hadn't seen him play solitaire in weeks, perhaps even months. He was usually too drunk to even shuffle a deck.

Could it be that the fog was finally starting to lift?

She muffled the tiny quiver of hope. She could not afford any more foolish fantasies.

She opened the front door to find her usual maid accompanied by another woman, slightly older but just as plain, and holding a dress box.

"*Bonsoir, mademoiselle*," the woman said in a dull, toneless voice. "My name is Berthelise. I'm here to help you get ready while Margot cleans and tends to the fires."

Violette frowned. "Margot usually takes care of both."

"Monsieur Estienne insisted. He thought I would do a better job as your lady's maid."

A shudder ran down Violette's spine and gripped her gut. This woman was under the Boneman's direct orders. Not

Lenoir's. Her heart knocked painfully against her rib cage.

"Very well. Come in."

Emile barely looked up at the visitors and continued to flip his cards. "Are you working tonight, then?"

"Yes, I suppose so." Surely a new dress meant Lenoir would take her somewhere teeming with wealthy patrons. Unless it wasn't Lenoir... Unless, tonight, it was someone else.

"Not working," Berthelise said. "Monsieur Estienne has requested your presence at a banquet hosted by a friend of his at the Place Vendôme."

Place Vendôme? Whoever this friend was, he must be both highly born and obscenely wealthy. Her stomach plummeted further. A great fortune in the wrong hands bred disaster.

"That... That is most generous of him."

"Monsieur Estienne can be very generous indeed. Would you like to see your new dress?"

Violette nodded and led Berthelise to her room. With each step, her legs wobbled. *Just one more step. Just one more.*

Berthelise set the box on the bed and opened the lid, parting rustling paper to reveal dark blue velvet, deep as the night sky. Berthelise withdrew a smaller box and snapped it open. White rhinestones on black satin sparkled in the candlelight.

Berthelise kept her listless eyes fixed on Violette. "This is a pretty necklace, is it not? The master has always known how to reward good behavior. There is nothing to fear, so long as one does as one is told. He has even been known to forgive a mistake, so long as it is swiftly and irrevocably corrected."

She snapped the little box shut. Blood pounded in Violette's ears and the bitter taste of panic rose in her throat, but she forced her body to remain perfectly still.

Estienne knew. Who had told him? How could she warn Nicolas? Oh God, if anything happened to him...

Don't think of that now. Do what you must—get through this evening, live to see the dawn of a new year. The Boneman had spared her so far. If she gave him the slightest reason to believe he stood to lose more by keeping her alive, she was done for.

"Come, *mademoiselle*, let us get you dressed. Monsieur Estienne asked that you look your very best tonight."

Violette nodded. "Of course."

He was not the first person who wanted her beautiful and docile. In fact, that was all anyone had ever asked of her, until Nicolas. What was one more evening pretending?

Once Violette was dressed and ready to go, Berthelise dogged her every footstep toward the door. Emile paused in shuffling the cards and looked up. For a fleeting moment, something passed through his eyes. Sadness? Regret? But then he turned his attention back to his game.

"Have a pleasant evening, brother," she murmured.

He merely grunted. Berthelise wrapped a shawl around her shoulders and nudged Violette forward, following her down the stairs. Apparently, her lady's maid was also going to escort her all the way to the Place Vendôme.

It could have been worse. The Boneman could have accompanied her in the fiacre. But no, he was simply waiting at their destination, one of the splendid *hôtel particuliers* with high windows and classic soaring lines, built in perfect symmetry around the square.

She'd never seen Estienne in evening wear before, but no tailored jacket, starched shirt or silk waistcoat was enough to make up for his pale, angular face and gaunt figure. When the skin stretched over his teeth in a grin, her stomach clenched with disgust.

His gaze swept over her. "The very picture of refinement. Monsieur de Cransac will be most pleased."

She kept her eyes firmly on her feet as they moved toward the entrance. *Just one more step. Just one more. Get through the night.* "Our host?"

"Indeed, and he is most eager to meet you," he replied in a falsely honeyed tone. "A well-born, genteel, unspoiled young woman such as yourself is a rare commodity."

Lord help her, that was all she was. A commodity being led to a particularly fancy marketplace.

"That is, if you are still unspoiled after that little stint you pulled with that whoreson Lefevre," he continued, his voice hardening. "If not, you had better tell me right now, because I assure you my client will be able to tell the difference."

Her legs nearly gave way. *Oh God.* Oh God, what was she about to…

Estienne smirked. "Rest assured, pet. If Monsieur de Cransac wants the rest of you, he's going to have to pay up first. Now put a smile on that pretty face and let's see if you're worth all the trouble you've caused me."

"Let us drink to the year ahead. Good health and good fortune to our families and friends. *Santé!*"

Jerome raised his glass, and Nicolas followed suit before taking a sip of wine. Pouilly-Fumé, a perfect white to accompany breaded sole and green beans in bechamel sauce. Yet as succulent as dinner promised to be, he wasn't hungry. It was as if his appetite for food and drink had dulled, overshadowed by a far greater craving that he couldn't satisfy.

He glanced at the other guests—no more than a dozen, and he'd met some of them at Jerome and Stella's table in the past. The mix of architects, musicians, and artists made for stimulating conversation. Truly, he couldn't think of a more pleasant way to celebrate the New Year, with an exquisite meal in front of him, a fire roaring on the hearth, and laughter and lively discussions ringing in his ears.

But the thorn in his side constantly reminded him of its presence, and his mind kept circling back to it. Where was Violette? Why hadn't she come back for their lessons? One day might have been fine. The second was worse. By the third, he had to wonder.

Had she been caught?

Dread filled his chest like ice-cold water whenever he thought of the danger she might be in. He'd sent a note to Malenfant, giving him sparse information about Violette and Lenoir, not enough to be of much use to him. Could someone have intercepted it? So far, he had one fraying lifeline to cling to. Suzanne's friend had spotted her with Bravard the evening after she'd fled the shop.

After she'd fled from *him*. Devil take it, how could he have let himself get carried away like that?

She kissed you. She asked you to kiss her. Took your hand and guided it up her leg. A scene he'd repeated in his head over and over again, and would do well not to think of now if he didn't want to embarrass himself. Yes, Violette's desire was unmistakable, raw in its intensity, a mirror of his own.

But it didn't make what they'd done any less foolish and reckless.

He took another gulp of wine and dug into his sole. Since when was he concerned with being reckless? Perhaps he was turning into a bourgeois. On the other hand, Violette risked more than he.

Damn it all, where is she?

After dinner, they retreated to the library for cognac and card games. Nicolas settled onto the divan and sipped the smooth, spicy liquor as he watched the flames dance in the hearth.

Jerome folded his hulking frame to sit beside him with a contented sigh. In the firelight, his reddish hair turned almost scarlet. "Nothing like a warm hearth when it's freezing outside."

Nicolas nodded. "Indeed."

His friend waited a moment before continuing. "You've been usually taciturn tonight. I thought you'd be regaling our guests with scandalous tales of the underbelly of Paris."

Nicolas raised an eyebrow. "Is that the only reason you invited me? You could tell quite a few stories yourself, old fellow."

Jerome's mouth quirked up in a wry smile. "I have no idea

what you're talking about. I am but a humble architect."

Nicolas almost laughed. "One only need look at the company you keep to know that's a bald-faced lie. That Marbois chap you sent my way…"

"Ah, so he got in touch with you? I knew your plan for a gymnasium and *savate* ring would pique his interest."

"Yes, seeing a fight where one man ended up with his shin-bone nearly sticking out of his leg quite piqued his interest. Marbois may dress like a proper gentleman, but it seems he has a taste for danger."

"You two should get along splendidly, then."

Nicolas swirled the cognac in his glass. Right now, perhaps for the first time, he understood the appeal of a safe, sheltered life.

Because he could keep *her* safe.

Jerome eyed him and frowned. "There must be something else."

"I don't want to spoil this delightful evening with my troubles," Nicolas simply replied. "Let us speak of happier things. Stella was magnificent in *Cosi Fan Tutte*."

"She is always magnificent." Jerome gazed at his wife across the room. She was at the card table playing a loud, spirited game of *belotte* with three other guests, her mouth curved into a brilliant smile and her dark gaze shining with mirth. "But I'm glad you enjoyed her performance."

"I will not soon forget it." All the more because he'd met Violette that night. A blessing and a curse.

"Good, because she'll soon be taking time away from the stage. Just for a few months."

Jerome's expression, the way his eyes danced with pride as they remained fixed on his wife, was all the explanation Nicolas needed. Stella was with child. For the first time that evening, the weight lifted entirely from his chest.

"Congratulations to you both, my friend." They clinked their glasses. "When is the happy event due?"

"June. Stella is beside herself with joy, of course. And we

were both eager for Clara to have a little brother or sister, though she already has a myriad of cousins."

One of which was the newborn son of Nicolas's dear friend Guy de Cazal and his wife Antonia, Jerome's sister. The memory of Nicolas's first meeting with Guy floated to the surface of his mind. Guy had been little more than a drunken wretch back then, freshly returned from exile, spending his family's fortune in the haunts of Palais Royal.

Two years later, he was a husband and a father, working tirelessly to provide for his wife and child. Anyone who saw him with Antonia would not doubt for a second that he would do anything to ensure her happiness.

Providing and protecting. Nicolas had always avoided any entanglement that might force him to assume such a role. Widows in possession of their own fortunes, older women with experience who had no room in their lives for anything more than a fleeting tryst, all of them made for pleasurable company without the responsibility that came with seducing a younger woman, especially if she was a virgin.

Laurine won't want to bed another man, ever, I can tell you that. I was the first one to touch her. A girl thinks that means something, you know? Like you're married or something. No, she won't go spreading her legs for anyone else, unless I order her to.

He'd witnessed the disastrous consequences when one failed to protect and provide. And since meeting Violette, he'd been increasingly unable to fend off the memories of Laurine. Memories that slithered in the cracks of the walls he'd built around himself, taunting him, whispering to him that he might fail again.

Maybe he already had.

"I will never be able to repay you, Nicolas." Jerome's voice broke through his thoughts. "Without your help, Stella would have been lost to me."

Nicolas shook his head. "Please, let us speak no more of it. You don't owe me anything."

"Be that as it may, whatever is tormenting you, I'm here to

return the favor if I can."

What if he took Jerome up on his offer? Maybe if he could find Violette and bring her here, or to Guy and Antonia's estate in the countryside… But no, it would only make things worse. The Boneman would hunt Violette down, no matter where she was. And Nicolas would make that madman aware of still more people he cared about.

"You could always try to find out if Marbois plans on investing in the gymnasium," he finally replied. "That would be most helpful."

Jerome nodded. "You can count on me."

An hour later, Nicolas bid his goodbyes to his friends. He wasn't the least bit tired, in fact he was fairly teeming with desperate energy. If Violette truly was in danger, he had wasted enough time already. But what was to be done at this hour? He couldn't well search every party or dinner in town for her. Better get some sleep, and then tomorrow… Tomorrow he'd find a way to reach her.

He decided against taking a fiacre. Castellane street to the Palais Royal wasn't a long walk, and breathing in the cold air helped clear his head. But the city was in no mood to sleep either. People spilled out from the crowded cabarets and cafés onto the pavement, staggering drunkenly and bellowing songs. If he wasn't so damn tired, he'd drop by the Cabaret Doré to see if Suzanne and Raoul were still there, perhaps have a few drinks himself.

As he reached the arcades of the Palais Royal, a voice rang out. "M'sieur Lefevre!"

A small boy with skinny legs ran up. No mistaking that high-pitched voice and that large wool hat.

"Albert, what the devil are you doing here?" Nicolas asked. "And at this hour?"

"M'sieur Prevost sent me to get you." The boy paused to suck in a breath. "Told me to wait for you here when you came back."

Nicolas's insides clenched. "What is it? What's wrong?"

"It's Saint Aphrodise, *m'sieur*. It's on fire."

Chapter Twelve

THE FLAMES SWIRLED high into the night, as if trying to reach the sky, and bathed the square in a crimson glow. Nicolas tilted his neck and watched, awestruck, unable to say a word or move a muscle.

What could be said? What could be done? Nothing. Not a bloody damn thing.

"By the time we heard there was a fire, it had already reached the roof. Best the brigade can do now is make sure it doesn't spread."

He tore his eyes from the flames' eerie dance. Raoul stood next to him, breathing hard, hair slicked down with sweat on his forehead. The firemen, yes. Pumping water onto the facades of the surrounding houses. Not on Saint Aphrodise. It was done for. The stone walls might hold even when the roof caved in, but only charred wood and blackened tiles would remain inside. It would simply be a ruin now, waiting for the authorities to raze it.

The acrid smell of burning wood filled his throat and lungs. The ring, the ropes, the sacks of straw. All he had when he'd started to train students. He'd made his own fortune since then, had gained access to higher circles of society. Yet all of it was flash, whereas Saint Aphrodise was solid stone. Gone now, up in smoke.

Suzanne laid a hand on his shoulder and he flinched. "You'll start again, Nicolas. We'll help you. And soon you'll have much better facilities, I'm certain of it."

Her voice was kind and soft, but any comfort she might have brought was swept away with the rising flames. Pure, destructive rage festered in his gut like an infected wound, and now it was open again, making him feel like a wild, wounded animal ready to lash out.

Estienne must have done this. There was no other explanation. Some drunken lout might have happened to drop a lantern inside, but the chances were far too slim. Violette had disappeared, now this… It had to be him. Coming from that twisted bastard, it was an almost friendly warning. *Don't tamper with my property, or I'll tamper with yours. Happy New Year!*

If Estienne had set fire to Saint Aphrodise in retaliation, that meant Violette was held captive. And the next time Nicolas crossed him, it wouldn't just be an old church burning. The Boneman had far more gruesome ways to send a message.

He turned away, his throat tightening until he struggled for a gulp of air. He couldn't leave Violette in the hands of that monster another second, and yet whatever he did would put her and his friends into still graver danger.

He was trapped. Hands tied. He could only watch helplessly as, all around him, Estienne sowed chaos.

First Laurine, and now…

No. No, he would not let it happen again. He curled his hand into a fist and pounded the wall of the building in front of him.

"Nicolas," Raoul growled. "No use doing this to yourself. Come now, let us go somewhere else."

"I need to do something," Nicolas grated. "*Anything.* I can't bear to let that whoreson destroy whatever he pleases on a whim."

"Right," Suzanne said. "We'll come up with a plan that doesn't involve mangling your own hand by punching the wall. But not here."

She gently slid her arm into his and led him away. The three of them made their way to Raoul's shop. Locked in the backroom, seated at the table in the soft glow of a lantern, Nicolas felt like he could once again breathe properly. Breathe and think.

Raoul crossed his arms. "I know you don't want to hear this, but we cannot bring down the Boneman by ourselves. We need Malenfant's help."

Nicolas shook his head. "No, I've just started repaying my debt to him. There has to be another way."

Suzanne leaned forward, her expression unusually stern. "First things first. You want to find Violette, don't you?"

He nodded. No need in telling her the thought of Violette had blotted out every other concern for the past three days. Sharp as she was, Suzanne may have guessed that on her own.

"I have no more sympathy for Malenfant than you," she continued.

"Really? Your cousins work for him."

She snorted. "And a rotten lot they are, same as him. Still, it'll be quicker that way. Malenfant has fewer men working for him than the Boneman but far more connections that could inform us of her whereabouts. You've already told him what you know about Violette, that makes finding her even easier."

"Suzanne is right," Raoul grumbled. "Just the three of us won't get very far with the Boneman hunting us down."

"It shouldn't be the three of us," Nicolas said. "You two should steer clear of me for the time being. If anything should happen to you…"

"Ha!" Suzanne laughed. "I've survived in the Palais Royal longer than you have, pretty boy. My choice of friends is my business."

"When we lived in Marseille, we faced almost certain death half a dozen times together," Raoul added. "What's once more? As long as we're not racing headlong into an early grave. Without Malenfant's help, you would have never taken down the

Kingfisher. You wouldn't have even tried, because you're not an idiot."

Damn him, but Raoul was making far too much sense. Nicolas sighed. "You're right. I'll pay Malenfant a visit first thing in the morning. Though I know full well what he's going to ask in return."

Loyalty. Allegiance. The very things he'd vowed to avoid. After that night Estienne and Lenoir had tied him up and made him watch…

I'll never be under anyone's orders, ever again.

He'd told Raoul those very words when they'd met. Even if it meant staying in exile on the other side of the country, far from Paris, he would stay free, unfettered, with no master to order him what to do. And when he had returned, he was strong enough to live by his own rules.

Now his principles paled in the face of what he was up against. Not only Estienne himself, but the idea of losing Violette forever. No, he couldn't risk it. Even if it meant renouncing his own freedom.

CLINK.

Violette's eyes shot open, and she scrambled to a sitting position, heart pounding. The brocade bed cover was scratchy beneath her fingers. She tried to swallow, but her mouth was dry. The door opened a crack and let in a sliver of light.

She could make out the silhouette of a servant on the other side. The girl set a platter on the floor without a word, then closed the door again. Locking it shut.

Clink.

Violette lay back on the cold mattress and hugged her knees. Her empty stomach was tied in a painful knot, and the thought of food brought nothing but a wave of disgust. Besides, how was she supposed to eat in the pitch darkness? Did Cransac think she was some sort of animal?

Obviously yes, since he was keeping her locked up. How long had she been there? The sky was beginning to lighten when she'd been taken to the room. Estienne himself had escorted her there, fingers digging into her arm, and pushed her roughly inside. She'd slept, uneasily, the slightest noise calling her awake. One hour? Six? Impossible to tell.

Was Cransac still drunkenly haggling over her price with the Boneman before coming to claim his due? Estienne had done his bit, parading her in front of that horrid man and his wealthy guests as they downed glass after glass of champagne and liquor. Men clad in the finest silks, their hair slick with pomade or covered with curly wigs. Ladies with garish rouge on their cheeks and lips, colorful plumes in their hair, glittering jewelry dripping down their cleavage to their low-cut necklines. Mistresses, of course. No wife would ever dare show herself in public in such scandalous attire.

She touched the rhinestones around her neck. Her fingers tightened around the necklace and anger boiled to the surface. She ripped it off and flung it into the darkness. It fell to the ground with a tinkle.

Damn him to hell. Damn them *all* to hell. She would sooner burn the place to the ground than let Cransac touch her. Maybe she should, and let herself burn along with it.

None of that. You must think of another way. You must get out.

But how? She'd been led up to the third floor of Cransac's house. If she devised some way to escape from the window, she'd either break both her legs or be spotted immediately. As for escaping from the inside …

Where will you go? The Boneman will find you, and he'll kill Emile.

She squeezed her eyes shut against upwelling tears. Giving in would be so much easier. Exhaustion settled over her, heavier than lead. If only she could fall asleep and never wake up.

She sank back into a fitful slumber. Woke again to the noise of the lock.

This time, light flooded the room almost immediately. Two servants entered, one holding a lantern and a stack of clothes, the other a large pitcher.

"Master said you're to clean yourself and wear this," the first girl said.

She set the lantern down and spread out a white nightrail with lace ruffles and ribbons.

The knot in her gut clenched. "Is this a jest? Why would he want me to wear this?"

Certainly, he didn't want her to have a good night's sleep. The way he'd leered at her... It was as if his gaze had left a viscous film over her skin.

The servant shrugged. "He gave us our orders and went right back to bed. Megrim. Might be awhile until he's up."

Unsurprising, given how foxed he'd been. "What is the time?"

"Three hours past noon."

The other servant poured water into a porcelain basin in a corner of the room. Violette stood and the first girl undressed her and took the pins out of her hair. After she'd washed herself, she slipped on the lacy nightrail. The servants left, but the lantern remained.

Violette sat on the edge of the bed and glanced around the room. Wallpaper printed with pineapples and exotic flowers, gold leaf on the furniture, the posts of the bed of solid oak. Opulent, just like what little she'd seen of the house. Even the nightrail felt as if it were made of the softest, lightest muslin.

Easy to tear off. The thought filled her head to toe with icy dread. What was the point of dressing her if that's not what Cransac intended to do?

Think. There must be a way out.

Hour after hour, her mind whirled fruitlessly as she lay on the bed and stared at the velvet canopy, then got up to open the window and test the bolts on the shutters. Again and again, as if they would somehow open if she tried enough times. But it was no use. There was no open window, no hidden door in the walls.

She had no means of reaching out for help, nothing she could bargain with.

Would Emile notice her absence? Would he worry, seek help? No, she could not expect anything from him. He couldn't even look after himself.

Nicolas…

She covered her face with her hands. She couldn't bear to think of him now. She should have stayed with him instead of fleeing. Stayed in the warmth of his arms, his golden beauty and low, murmured words stoking everything that was alive and vivid and true within her.

Perhaps if she could convince one of the servants to pass a message, to help her escape…

The thud of heavy footsteps and creaking floorboards sent blood pounding in her ears, and all her thoughts vanished. She bolted to her feet.

The door opened to reveal Cransac. Good Lord, he looked even more revolting without his wig. His thinning hair and the dark circles lining his eyes made his pudgy face distinctively toad-like.

"Come closer," he said. "Let's have a look at you."

She took a small step forward, hands curling into fists under the lace edge of her sleeves.

"Scared of me, are you?" He shook his head and snorted. "You're good at playing the frightened virgin, I'll give you that. But I want to make sure I got what I paid for."

What did he mean by that? She stood perfectly still with a strange energy coursing through her limbs.

"I'm going to have someone examine you properly," he added. "Blast, I'm in no state to enjoy much of anything with this bloody headache in any case."

He retreated toward the door and stopped to look at the platter that still lay untouched on the floor. "Eat your food. I won't have you fainting or flopping around like a dead fish. I like it better when a girl has a little fight in her, and Estienne told me you had plenty."

Clink.

She let out a breath. A reprieve. A short one, perhaps, but she would take what she could get.

Chapter Thirteen

A SHIVER RAN over Violette's skin, and she curled in on herself under the covers, chasing warmth and clinging to the last shreds of her dream. A hand clasping hers, urging her to run, to escape through a long, dark tunnel… Someone she trusted instinctively, but sleep receded before she could make out who it was.

She opened her eyes. Shivers wracked her and her stomach rumbled. The servants had lit a fire in the hearth before she'd gone to bed but it had now gone cold. Was it morning? If so, she'd been locked in here for a full day. How long before Cransac came back?

Footsteps answered her question. Pushing aside the dread that threatened to weigh her down, she sat and threw back the covers.

The door opened, and the light of lantern flooded the room as one of the servants entered.

The urge to try something, anything, burst within Violette, obliterating rational thought. She leaped from the bed. "Please… Please, I need to send a letter. If you could—"

The girl didn't even meet her gaze. She simply set the lantern down on the nightstand before holding the door open.

"She's in there. Be quick about it, you hear?"

Cransac. Violette took a step back and curled her fingers around the bedpost. Cransac led in an elderly woman wearing a plain wool dress. The woman eyed Violette with a sharp, keen gaze, her wrinkled mouth set in a grim line.

Cransac crossed his hands over his belly. "I trust you slept well, my dear." He turned to the servant. "Did you make sure she ate?"

The girl nodded, and Violette tightened her grip on the post. Last night she'd been unable to stop herself from eating some bread and a small piece of cheese. The demands of her empty stomach had been too pressing, as if her body was stubbornly intent on maintaining its strength even when all hope for escape seemed lost.

"Very well," Cransac added. "Leave us now, and shut the door."

Find a way. It's not over yet.

"How old are you?" the old woman asked once the servant had gone.

Violette remained silent.

"Answer her, damn you, or I'll beat you bloody before we even start," Cransac grumbled.

Hateful, repugnant man. Fury sparked and spread within her, but she forced herself to keep it under control. *Think. Don't act rashly.*

"One and twenty," she replied between gritted teeth.

"When are your courses due?" the old woman continued.

Violette glared at her. What the devil did it matter? She forced herself to remember the last time her courses came. "Not for two weeks yet."

"Good. Lie down and spread your legs."

Her heart sprang in her chest and beat erratically against her rib cage. "What? Are you mad?"

A smug smile twisted Cransac's lips. "Come now, it won't take a minute. Need to make sure I'm getting my money's worth."

The woman advanced on Violette and grasped her wrist. Grey-haired though she was, her grip was firm and unyielding.

"It'll hurt more if you struggle. Believe me, I've done this often enough."

Violette pulled at her arm. "Unhand me!"

"Stupid little twit," the woman yelped. "You keep that up, and I'll ask the servants to pin you down while we take a look at your cunt. Is that what you want?"

Her fury burst free. "I said, *unhand me!*"

She let go of the post and tightened her fingers into a fist. *Between the ribs. Do it. Now.*

Her knuckles met the hollow in the old woman's chest and hit bone. Much easier to aim without a blindfold. The woman's breath came out in a whoosh, and she crumpled to the floor, gasping for air. Violette tore free and ran toward the door.

"You filthy harlot!" A meaty arm wrapped around her waist. "You're mine, you hear?"

She struggled against him, trying to break free and reach the door, but he was too heavy. He slammed her against the floor, and all the air left her lungs.

"Would you rather we do it this way?" he barked. "Damn you to hell, I'll take a chance at deflowering you myself right here."

She sucked in a gulp of air. A voice resounded in her head, cutting through the red haze of panic. *Make your enemy underestimate you. Lead him to expect one move and then…*

"I beg of you," she whimpered. "Please, don't hurt me."

"Oh, you're begging now?" He loomed over her. "I should teach you a proper lesson so you know when to shut your mouth and when to open it."

She covered her face with her arms. *"Please,* I'll do whatever you want, I promise."

Cransac smirked. "That's better. Now be a good girl and—"

A single sharp kick between the legs cut him off cold. Right where Suzanne had taught her to hit. Hard. He doubled over and she scrambled to her feet. Kicked him again. Then ran to grab the lantern from the nightstand, and flung it at his face.

Run. Run now.

She burst into the corridor. They'd led her up to the room by the grand staircase. She bolted in the opposite direction. Staring straight ahead, not looking back to see if anyone was following her. *The stairs. Find the servants' stairs.*

How would she even get out? The door would be locked. Someone would see her. She was barefoot, in her nightgown, and it was freezing outside. She wouldn't get far.

Don't think. Just run.

At the end of the corridor a door lay half hidden in the wall panels. A servant's door. She pried it open with her fingers and reached a darkened staircase.

She hurried down the cold stone steps, arms outstretched to feel for the banister and the wall. *Hurry. Faster.* She tripped, caught herself, started down again.

And bumped into a large, solid body. A scream tore from her throat but a large hand clamped over her mouth to smother it.

"What the devil?" a low voice growled in the darkness.

A shuffling behind him betrayed the presence of another person. "A servant? Coming down without a lantern?"

Nicolas.

It couldn't be. But it was. She would recognize the smooth tone of his voice anywhere. She shook her head frantically against the other man's hand.

"If you start screaming again, it'll be the last thing you do, you understand?"

She nodded and the man released her. "Nicolas," she breathed. "It's me."

"*Sacredieu,*" he cursed. "Let's get out of here, Talloche. Hurry."

How had he found her? And who was this other man? No matter. Her body reeled with the need to get out of this horrid place, and she followed them, half-racing half-staggering down the stairs.

At the bottom, the door hung open, the lock smashed in. Two bodies lay on the ground, and the faint light of dawn coming from outside caught a pool of dark liquid on the paved floor.

Finally, they were out. Cold cut through her skin like blades. And she could see Nicolas now, his broad shoulders, his blond curls. He turned and caught her hand. Relief jolted through her, so strong it made her head spin. She squeezed his fingers. Yes, he was really there, leading her across the Place Vendôme to a waiting fiacre.

The other man—Talloche—bounded up to next to the driver and Nicolas slammed the door open, helping her inside. As soon as he'd closed it again, the carriage barreled off.

"Are you hurt?" Nicolas panted.

"I... I..."

She stared down at her feet. They were wet. Burning with the cold. She hadn't even noticed until now.

"Devil take it, you're barefoot. And freezing." He took off his coat and draped it over her. "Here, bundle up close to close to me. It'll keep you warm until we reach our destination at least."

She nodded absently. She still couldn't speak. It was all too much. Relief warred with dread as the realization of what she'd done washed over her.

"Emile," she said. "We have to find my brother. As soon as the Boneman hears about this..."

Nicolas wrapped his arm around her shoulders and brought her closer to him, enveloping her in his warmth. "Malenfant is taking care of it."

"Malenfant? You're working with him?"

"Do not trouble yourself with that." His tone was soothing, but carried an edge. "All that matters is that you're safe now."

Safe. Emotion rose up within her like a gathering tide and spilled out onto her cheeks. Her throat tightened and expelled a sob.

"Did Cransac harm you?" Nicolas asked, his voice wavering

slightly. "If he did, I swear I will go back and gut him like a pig."

She shook her head. "He didn't have a chance. He… I managed to fight him off. I remembered what you taught me."

Nicolas's thumb brushed the wetness of her cheek. "I have never been prouder of any student." He pressed his lips against her forehead. "Now you must recuperate. We will arrive shortly, and then you can rest."

Chapter Fourteen

NICOLAS PEERED OUT the window, as the fiacre rumbled across the cobblestones. The sky was lightening, and already people were out in the streets of the Palais Royal, setting up stalls or unloading carts of supplies for the shops. Good thing they were a stone's throw from his apartments. He didn't want Violette out too long in the freezing weather, and where anyone could see her.

She was still curled against him, hugging her knees, covered in his coat. Wearing nothing but that horrible lacy nightrail. A disguise to make her look more virginal. Wasn't that why that *débauché* had bought her in the first place?

She'd fought Cransac off before he'd had time to hurt her. Still, he'd laid his hands on her. Humiliated her. Treated her no better than a thing to play with.

Dark rage swirled in his gut and rose with such force that he had to tighten and release his fists to calm the trembling in his limbs. The need to hurt, to crush, to kill lashed within like a ferocious, caged animal. If he and Talloche had gone all the way to Cransac's bedchamber to rescue Violette, his knife would have ended in the bastard's belly, buried to the hilt. Perhaps the sight of blood on his fancy carpets would have satisfied Nicolas's thirst for vengeance.

Violette looked up and locked her gaze with his. She wasn't smiling, but her eyes were soft. Luminous. His heart thumped hard in his chest, and this time it wasn't out of anger.

He'd found her. She was here, safe in his arms. Far from the Boneman and Cransac and Lenoir and anyone else who wanted to hurt her. *Not far enough.* But it would do for now, and he wouldn't let her out of his sight.

The fiacre slowed and stopped in front of the row of arcades that formed the southern gallery.

"Wait here," he told Violette. "I have to speak to Talloche. I won't be long."

She nodded, almost sleepily. By God, she must be exhausted. And he wouldn't be quite able to breathe easily until she was curled in his bed, sleeping soundly. Where he himself would sleep… No use speculating on it now. All in good time.

He opened the door and climbed out of the fiacre. Talloche jumped from his perch next to the driver and stretched his neck.

"Damn it to hell, I sooner would have walked from the Place Vendôme," he grumbled. "Well, we got the girl, so that's settled."

Nicolas frowned. His debt to Malenfant was hardly settled. No, he was well and truly caught in the man's web now. But Raoul was right, he never would have found Violette, or at least not so quickly, without that blackguard's help. And time in this case had been of the essence.

"What now?" he asked Talloche. "Is there a ceremony where I kneel, kiss Malenfant's ring, and swear my allegiance?"

Talloche laughed. "Malenfant doesn't give a rat's arse about pomp and ceremony. Says he got enough of that in church. He was a choir boy when he was a lad, believe it or not."

Nicolas raised an eyebrow. "I admit I'm leaning towards *not.*"

"What he cares about is money. Gold. Fine things. Power is just a way to get those. And as soon as he has a mission for you that can bring in more, he'll let you know."

Nicolas nodded shortly. "And about Violette's brother…"

Finding Emile was just as important as finding Violette,

something he'd insisted on when he'd discussed the situation with Malenfant. Emile was the only reason the Boneman had a hold on her. But when Malenfant's men turned up at their apartment yesterday, he was gone. All they'd found was a woman lying on the floor, with a bloody bruise to her temple and a candlestick next to her head.

"He'll let you know as well," Talloche said. "The two men he sent on the job are good hunters."

"All right. I'll wait for news, then."

He returned to Violette and took her hand to help her out of the fiacre. His gaze landed on her bare foot, white against the dark wood of the step. He placed his hand on her shoulder to stop her movement.

"You're not walking all the way to my apartment without shoes. Out of the question."

"Oh." Her cheeks tinged with red. "Well…"

"Come on, then."

He pulled her to him and hooked his arm beneath her knees, lifting her against his chest. Her blush deepened, but she circled his neck with her arms nonetheless. Heavens, she was light as a bird. Carrying her up the stairs to the second floor hardly gave him any trouble. Starting now, he would have to make sure she was eating to her heart's content.

He set her down gently and knocked on the door. Pierre, his manservant, opened immediately and stepped aside to let them in.

"You have a domestic?" Violette murmured.

"Yes. And a housekeeper. The best use of money one can make is to employ honest people."

He took the coat from her shoulders and handed it to Pierre. Bless the man, his expression remained unfailingly polite, just as it always did when Nicolas brought home company, though the present circumstances were quite peculiar, even for him.

Nicolas placed a hand on the small of Violette's back and led her to the sitting room. Her gaze darted from the high windows to the cherry wood wainscotting topped with cerulean wallpaper and chairs upholstered in gold and leafy green.

"Heavens, it's so colorful."

He smiled. "You haven't noticed I favor color? I thought my waistcoats would have given me away."

"No, it's just…" She hugged herself. "Perhaps I'm no longer used to seeing much color. Emile and I had to sell almost all our furniture to get by."

Blast, he would have to tell her about Emile sooner or later. If only he could pretend, just for a few hours, that the outside world no longer existed… But no, pushing it back would only make things worse.

He took her hand, and they sat on the divan. "Listen, I asked Malenfant to send some men to fetch your brother."

Her fingers trembled in his, and she swallowed. "Did they… Did they find him?"

"They didn't. He was gone. We're not sure what happened. They found a woman lying unconscious on the floor, hit with a candlestick—"

Her gaze sharpened. "A woman? What did she look like?"

Nicolas repeated what Malenfant's man had told him. "Brown hair. Neither young nor old. Dressed in a plain dress, but without an apron or a servant's cap."

She frowned. "It could have been Berthelise."

The name rang in his mind like a gun shot. "Did you say Berthelise? Berthelise Arthaud is one of Estienne's most notorious agents. I've never met her, thank God, or I might not have lived to tell the tale. She's an expert at infiltrating houses, passing herself off as a servant, but she'll slit your throat without a moment's hesitation."

"So Emile might have knocked her out and escaped." She shook her head. "How did he do it? Perhaps… Perhaps he wasn't as drunk and helpless as she thought."

"We won't know until they find him. And they *will* find him, Violette."

He squeezed her hand, and the ghost of a smile passed over her lips. "Yes. At least there's hope."

Hope. He'd never given the sentiment much thought. But sitting in his home with Violette, he found he did hope, desperately, achingly. There might still be a way out of this impossible situation.

"I'm going to ask my housekeeper to draw you a hot bath and prepare something to eat," he said. "Then you can go sleep if you wish."

She nodded and her teeth pulled at her lower lip, as if she wanted to ask him something but couldn't summon the nerve. He cleared his throat and inhaled a shaky breath. Good Lord, after all she'd been through, it was no wonder she was nervous.

And so was he. Another sentiment that had been alien to him until now.

"Take my bed, I'll sleep on the divan," he added quickly. "And if you prefer I'll ask Suzanne to come keep you company."

"No. It's fine." She laid a hand on his arm. "I trust you."

He stood. His pulse was pounding too quickly, and she was too near. Too damn near. Her hair, curling on her shoulders, her fresh floral scent… It was impossible to hold back the memory of what they'd done the other night, the way he'd held her and kissed her and let all his reserve fall away to bring them both the pleasure they sought.

He rose abruptly from the divan. "I'll see to your bath."

Better not give her the slightest hint that her trust might be misplaced.

WARM.

Violette smoothed her hands over the silk dressing gown. Sea green and soft against her skin, and so warm. She breathed in. It smelled like Nicolas—the clean, citrusy scent of bergamot. The fire roaring in the hearth, the plate of steaming food on the table, the lush carpet under her feet, she let all of it wash over her like the hot water of her bath and seep into her bones, as if it could make her forget forevermore the sensation of being cold.

She sat at the table in front of the plate of potatoes and chicken drowned in cream and mushroom sauce. She closed her eyes and inhaled the thick, earthy aroma before picking up her fork.

Nicolas sat across from her and smiled. *"Bon appétit.* You'll have to let me know if there are any particular dishes you enjoy."

She nodded, too ravenous to stop eating and reply. But Nicolas didn't seem to mind. He simply watched her, taking slow sips from a glass of wine, his hair shining like molten gold in the candlelight.

"You're not eating anything?" she finally asked, once she was done with half her plate.

"I usually don't eat much in the mornings. I build up my appetite when I practice."

"Will you be going to practice today?"

His smile faltered. "I'd rather not leave you alone if I can help it. Besides, circumstances make practicing rather difficult at present."

"What do you mean?"

He drained his glass and set it down on the table. "Saint Aphrodise burned down. Courtesy of the Boneman."

Suddenly, all that delicious food turned to lead in her stomach. Devil take it, the Boneman had done this because of *her.* "I don't know what to say. I... I'm so sorry, I never should have—"

"None of that," he interrupted her. "It would have happened sooner or later, given our history. I'm surprised it took so long, actually."

Our history. She hadn't dared ask before, but now her curiosity burned even stronger. "How do you know Estienne?"

Nicolas stared for a while at the flames dancing on the hearth.

"My mother died giving birth to me, and my brother and my father were executed during the Terror. We were hardly royalist, but they thought the Revolutionary Tribunal were nothing but a bunch of power-mad thugs, and made no secret of it. It cost them their heads."

She covered her mouth with her hand. To lose a loved one to the guillotine was horrid enough, but two... Had he witnessed the executions, lost in the crowd clamoring for blood? It didn't bear thinking about.

"Somehow, I managed to escape their net. I ended up at the Palais Royal, living on the streets, and then I met Lenoir. He was an orphan too. We were both sixteen, angry and hungry. We'd go around with other boys trying to sniff out *sans-culottes* or anyone who had been favorable to the Terror and beat them bloody."

"You were a *muscadin?*"

She'd heard about them, of course. Groups of young men who liked to wear flashy clothes and musky perfume, while running wild in the streets of Paris, getting into violent fights with revolutionaries.

Nicolas nodded and gave a dry, hollow laugh. "The only thing I still keep from that time is my taste in clothes. Back then, we were foolish enough to think we were dispensing justice, though it didn't take much for someone to end up with broken teeth or a knife wound. Then Estienne came along, and that changed. He became our leader, organized us into a proper gang. He wasn't the strongest, but he was the cruelest by far, and he had the sort of intelligence that made it easy for him to pinpoint anyone's weakness."

She shivered. She knew this firsthand. "He hasn't changed."

"No. If anything, he's gotten worse. Lenoir idolized him from the start, and that hasn't changed either." He sighed. "I could never see anything else in him than a villain. Estienne knew this, and he made me pay for it dearly. I... I had to leave Paris for a time."

"You went to Marseille." He looked at her, brows raised in surprise, and she continued. "Suzanne told me you'd met Raoul there. Then you came back with him."

"Paris is my home." His eyes blazed fiercely. "It always has been, and it always will be. I wasn't going to let Estienne keep me away from it. He wasn't too glad when I returned, of course, and he's never forgiven me for not being a good, loyal dog like Lenoir."

Violette waited for him to go on, but Nicolas nodded toward her plate. "Enough of this now. It's spoiling your appetite."

After what he'd just told her, food was the last thing on her mind. Nicolas had lost his family and had done what he could to survive, same as her and Emile. No, worse, because he had been left with nothing. And yet he hadn't ended up sick with drink, or wasting away in some gambling hell.

"How did you manage to build such a life for yourself, after what you've been through?"

The smile returned to his lips. "Life. That's it. I've been blessed with a great desire to live, and not only to survive. The Widow could make the streets run red with blood tomorrow, but at least I'll be sure I won't have spent my time on this earth cowering in fear and denying what makes each day a worthy pursuit."

She rose from her chair. His words, his smile, the glow of the hearth, the feel of the silk robe on her bare skin, all of it had lit a fire within her, the very same that had roared free the other night under his eager touch. She had survived for years, and yet only now was she truly beginning to live.

His smile vanished as she stepped around the table and to his chair, but desire lit his gaze. "Violette…"

"Do not speak," she murmured.

If he tried to dissuade her, to reason with her… No, she was done with prudence and reason. Nothing, no one, stood between them now. She wanted to feel it again, that crushing lust that had taken control of her, obliterating everything else.

She placed her hands on his shoulders and leaned down to kiss him. Nicolas moaned into her mouth and *oh*, his lips moved against hers, gently teasing them until they opened. The sensation drove straight to her core, throbbing, pulsing with each slick stroke of his tongue. His hands slid up the silk robe from her thighs to grip her waist.

"Is this truly what you want?" he rasped.

She nodded frantically. "Yes. Please, tell me you want the same."

An agonized groan rose from his throat. "I have wanted this since I first laid eyes on you."

Lord, the utter certainty with which he spoke it… She kissed him again, more hungrily now, and his clever fingers worked to undo the knot at her waist. When it gave way, her robe fell open. Nicolas's gaze raked over her body, leaving a flush of pure heat in its wake.

"Straddle me," he demanded.

She hesitated for a moment. Would it feel strange, being so… open and bare against him?

He lifted his hand to stroke her cheek. "I promise you, love, it will not be unpleasant for you. On the contrary."

She carefully placed her legs on either side of him and lowered herself to a sitting position.

"Oh, I… *oh*."

Her breath caught in her chest. The hard ridge beneath the falls of Nicolas's trousers pressed against her throbbing center, as if it had been made to arouse her most sensitive spot and drive her desire higher. Even the tiniest movement as she adjusted her position sent sparks of pleasure coursing through her body.

Nicolas grabbed her hips again, fingers digging into her flesh, and pulled them into a rolling movement. "You feel it, don't you? How good it is?"

She moaned, gripping his shoulders for balance. "God, yes, it's… Oh, what are you doing to me?"

He grinned. "I'm not doing anything. You're doing it to yourself. Go on, love, it'll only get better."

How could it possibly be better than this? She'd never felt such a powerful, consuming sensation in her life, as if she was going to catch fire at any moment. Then Nicolas's mouth latched on to her neck, nibbling and sucking, dragging his tongue along the curve, and she understood. Yes, she was catching fire, and yet the aching pulse wasn't satisfied yet. It wanted more, more pressure, more friction, more of his mouth and his hands and that solid bulge that fit so perfectly against her.

Nicolas slid the robe from her shoulders and trailed kisses down to her breasts. "My God, you're breathtaking," he murmured against her skin. "I want to give you so much pleasure, love, all the pleasure you deserve."

The tip of his tongue flicked her nipple, and a jolt of pleasure ran straight through her. She tossed her head back and whimpered. He did it again, again, again, swirling his tongue now, then taking her into his mouth in a greedy pull. She nearly sobbed at the sharp, exquisite heat his mouth spurred within. She rolled her hips back and forth, back and forth, chasing something that was just out of reach, but so close, so close…

Nicolas sucked harder, gripped tighter. Something inside her broke loose, burst into white-hot shards, coursed through her limbs in a whirlwind. A hoarse cry ripped from her chest, and she fell against him, limp and satiated, head spinning, all tension melting from her muscles.

This was… incredible. Astounding. How could such bliss exist?

Nicolas caressed her hair. "My beautiful Violette. Would you think me a terrible cad if I took you to bed now?"

She smiled against his neck. "Only if you plan on sleeping."

Chapter Fifteen

NICOLAS'S HEART THUMPED madly in his chest. He tried to even his breathing, but his body vibrated with need, and his cock strained painfully against his trousers.

"Take it off," he managed, "and get in bed."

The silk robe slid from Violette's shoulders and pooled on the floor. He sucked in a breath, and his gaze followed her, entranced, as she walked to the bed. Long legs, wide hips, but her torso was slight, her breasts small enough to fit in his palms, the rosy tips pointed, as if begging for his mouth to resume teasing them. Her skin, too, bore the mark of her arousal, its creamy whiteness contrasting with a lovely flush on her collarbones and cheeks.

Perfection. How was it possible that such a woman was trusting him with such a precious gift?

Fucking hell, he was nearly out of his mind for her. He'd lain with many beautiful women. Some of them far outmatched him when it came to bedroom skills, but every one of them paled in comparison to Violette, like paper lanterns next to a full moon.

And it wasn't just her body. Guy had once told him that virginity was merely a state of being rather than a state of mind, but Nicolas had never fully understood what he meant until tonight. Her skin seemed to ripple, as if passion simmered just beneath the surface before blazing under his touch and building to a shattering peak. Even through the cloth, he'd felt her clench against his cock. He'd never in his life been as hard, as needy with lust.

Damn it all, he'd fall to his knees and beg if she wished. But Violette wasn't here to play that sort of game. She stretched on the dark green velvet bedspread, stark desire burning her gaze as she watched him undress.

But when he pushed down his trousers and his cock finally sprang free, she frowned slightly and bit down on her lip. The last time he'd been with an inexperienced girl, he himself was young and green, nearly a decade ago. Back then he didn't have the slightest idea what he was doing, nor how to calm his partner's nervousness.

Violette, on the other hand… He couldn't bear thinking she might be apprehensive, not even a little. And it was up to him to make sure she wasn't.

He joined her on the bed, his breath shaky. *Be gentle. Smooth. Don't hurry.* Even if it felt like holding back a raging river. She pressed a hand to his chest, as if testing its firmness, then let her palm slide down to his belly, lightly stroking the trail of hair that led to his manhood, up and down, up and down. He bit back a groan. If she kept doing that, her introduction to the pleasures of the flesh was going to be dramatically short-lived.

She looked down at his cock and frowned. "I was told this would be painful."

He caught her hand and kissed it. "At first, yes. Until you get used to me. But in time, if I'm doing everything right, you should be able to reach the same peak that you just experienced."

Her eyes widened. "That's… possible? Feeling that way when you lie with a man?"

He almost laughed. "Why shouldn't it be?"

"My mother made it sound… thoroughly unpleasant. Tedious, almost. Just waiting with one's legs spread for it to be over."

Good Lord, the people who taught *aristo* girls about marital relations should be locked up in Bicêtre prison. He shook his head. "Let me show you, love. Then you'll know what to expect."

He kissed her. Stroked her hair, her neck, her breast, swirling his thumb over her nipple before squeezing softly. Violette moaned and arched against him, but he took his time, his hand inching lower to her belly, before finally reaching the soft tuft of hair between her legs.

"Now just lie back and let me touch you here," he murmured against her lips. "If it hurts, tell me so. I'll stop."

She nodded and closed her eyes. He gently parted her folds, still slick from the pleasure she'd taken on the chair, and delicately teased her entrance while pressing the base of his palm to her mound, right over her tender nub. She whimpered and her legs fell apart—slightly at first, then in earnest when he swirled his finger and dipped in the wet heat. Just a knuckle for now. No need to hurry. It was just like watching a flower open its petals.

"Do you like that?" he asked.

Her eyelids fluttered open. "Yes. *Yes*, go on."

His finger slid deeper, and her eyes squeezed shut again. Breathy sighs emerged from her lips each time he plunged, deeper and deeper still, following the rhythmic movement of her hips. They jerked up to meet him now, spurring him on, and the sighs turned to little cries. His cock was hard as stone, aching for release, blood pumping madly throughout his body. Devil take it, he couldn't wait any longer, and she was more than ready for him.

He pulled his hands away, and she groaned at the loss, face flushed, eyes opening to meet his in a pleading manner. He positioned himself over her and rubbed the head of his cock over her folds.

"Oh, that's... *Oh God*," she mewled. "Nicolas..."

Bloody fucking hell, when she said his name like that... It was miracle he didn't come on the spot. "I'm going to enter you now, same as I did with my fingers. This is where it can be painful, so I'll go as slow as you wish."

She nodded frantically. *"Please*, I... I want you inside me, I don't care if it hurts."

Her hands circled his torso, fingers digging into his lower back, urging him forward. He pushed. A wave of pleasure racked his body through and through. Heavens above, the feeling of her tight, slick sheath around him was more exquisite than anything he'd known, and he wasn't even fully inside her yet.

Limbs trembling, he rolled his hips. *Control your movements. Not too fast.* Blast, this was more strenuous than any *savate* match he'd known.

Violette winced, and he drew back instinctively. "No," she breathed. "Don't stop. I need you. Don't ever stop."

The fire within roared higher at her words. He jerked his hips more sharply, and she cried out. Pleasure or pain? She lifted her knees, hooking her legs around him, and drew him deeper. He couldn't think, couldn't slow down. Delicious tension built at the base of his manhood, tighter and tighter, closer to snapping with each thrust.

But if he could get her there again first...

He titled his pelvis to create more friction against her sensitive nub. This time, her cry was unmistakably one of pleasure, somewhere between a wail and a moan, and she clenched around him.

"God, that's so good, love," he panted. "So damn good. I'm going to come."

"More," she nearly sobbed. "Please, Nicolas..."

He plunged into her fully, holding nothing back as she reached her peak again, but he was already on the brink. He had to pull away, *now*. The tension snapped, and his seed spurted onto her belly in time with swells of pleasure rushing through his body. He let his head fall in the crook of her neck, breathing hard.

For a moment, she simply held him close, catching her own breath, stroking his hair.

"I understand now," she said in a small voice.

He rolled to his back and grinned at her. No victory, no fight, no win had ever felt so thrilling. "Understand what?"

She smiled. "Why mothers don't tell us it can be this good. We'd want to do it all the time."

He laughed and brushed her tousled hair back from her cheek. "Well, luckily, I have no plans today but seeing to your pleasure."

She kissed his palm, and her smile widened. Lord, her eyes were so bright, it nearly knocked the breath out of him again.

"If you don't mind, I'd like to finish my plate first. Perhaps this has whetted your appetite as well, just like *savate*?"

Indeed. Though he felt as if it might never be fully satiated again.

"I SHOULD NEVER have sent for your clothes. I like it you much better in nothing but my dressing gown."

Violette looked up from the book she was reading and leaned her head against the back of the divan. Nicolas turned up the points of his collar and slipped his cravat around his neck, his mouth curled into a dashing smile.

Her heart fluttered. Heavens, he cut such a handsome figure in his tailor-made breeches and tight waistcoat of blue silk brocade. But not so handsome that she didn't want him to take all of it off again so she could gaze upon his perfectly sculpted muscles and golden skin.

"I could say the same for you," she replied. "This is the first time I've seen you fully dressed for the past two days."

Or was it three? The hours were starting to form a sensual blur. Outside, tiny flakes drifted from dark gray clouds that turned daylight into dusk, and they hadn't left Nicolas's apartment since he'd brought her here.

Violette turned back to her book but found herself reading the same sentence over and over again. Not that the subject was particularly interesting to her. Nicolas owned a dozen books, all of them about naval history and famous battles of Antiquity. If she were to stay here longer...

As soon as the thought entered her mind, she tried to push back, but it wormed its way back to the forefront.

You have no money, no home. You depend on him now. What will happen a week from today? A month?

By God, she could hardly imagine, with the Boneman a lurking threat to them both, and Emile still on the run—hopefully, or else that meant he was cold in the ground. But she couldn't help but wonder what Nicolas would offer her, what he expected, if anything.

A kept woman. A mistress. The words rang out in her head in her mother's stern, disapproving voice.

Violette closed the book and glanced at Nicolas again. He was studying his reflection in the mirror over the hearth, fingers working deftly to tie his cravat into a simple knot. However many years she lived, she would never regret what had happened between. Better to be his mistress than any other man's lawful wife. The trust he inspired, the warmth of his embrace, the bone-crushing pleasure he brought her... Her cheeks flushed. Only this morning, he'd taken her right there on the divan, flipping her over and grabbing her hips before plunging into her from behind, and she'd pleaded for more with each vigorous thrust.

She was still sore from it, but that didn't keep her body from aching for him. The fire, the thirst, it never stopped. Still, they could not stay here forever. Sooner or later, they would have to go back out into the world.

He turned toward her and grinned, as if he'd felt her gaze on him. "What is it, love?"

The word rolled off his tongue so lightly and naturally. Was it a common term of endearment for him? Or did it mean more?

She couldn't possibly ask him. Not now, with everything they had to deal with. She opted for an easier question. "Are you going out?"

He finished his knot and gave it a little tap. "No, but Marbois might drop by later today. He wishes to speak to me about our plans for a proper gymnasium and *savate* ring, though I'll have to find something temporary in the meantime. I can't have my students practicing on cobblestones in the middle of winter."

"Maybe we could go out, just for a short while," she suggested. "A stroll around the Parc Monceau, for example. What harm could that do?"

He joined her on the couch and leaned in for a kiss. "None, I suppose. But do you even have proper attire for snowy weather?"

She sighed. "I've made do with my shawl until now. It's quite warm."

His gaze roamed over her, lingering on her hips and bosom. "We must have a new wardrobe made for you. Coats, shoes, dresses worthy of your beauty."

An image flashed through her memory, the women at Cransac's party bedecked in silks and jewels. Mistresses. Dolls dressed up in finery to show off how much their lovers could spend on them. She frowned. No, Nicolas would never treat her that way. He simply wanted to take care of her.

He lifted her chin with his finger. "Tell me what's troubling you, love."

She smiled. "It is nothing. I think I just need some fresh air."

"I'd rather put an expression of perfect, blissful content on your lovely face, fresh air be damned."

He kissed her again, and she let her hands slide up to his cravat to pull him closer. Heavy heat gathered in her breasts, in her belly, between her legs, deep in the hidden core that he knew so well how to tease and stroke and fill.

He gathered up her skirts to slip his hand underneath. "I'm telling you, we should forgo clothes altogether. I'll welcome Marbois as bare as the day I was born if I have to."

She laughed, and his mouth traveled down to her neck in playful nips and licks. Goodness, the wetness was already starting to gather, making her slick with want…

A knock sounded at the door.

"A message for you, sir," came Pierre's voice.

Nicolas stopped and called over his shoulder. "*Sacredieu*, can't it wait?"

"The boy who delivered it said it was urgent."

"Blast." Nicolas rose from the divan and smoothed his clothes. "Wait here, love, I'll be right back."

She straightened and brushed her skirts back into place. The door stood ajar, and low murmurs drifted in from the corridor. She rose and tiptoed to the door, her light steps muffled by the carpet. Eavesdropping was a nasty habit she should have done away with long ago, but what could be so urgent? Perhaps it was news of Emile? A painful knot formed in her stomach.

"… quick as I can, of course," Nicolas whispered.

"Yes, *monsieur*."

"And if anyone tries to break in, you take her to the staircase immediately, do you understand?"

The knot tightened. Lord have mercy, what was happening?

"You can count on me, *monsieur*."

"Good. Fetch me my coat."

She quickly padded back the divan. A moment later, Nicolas entered again. Smiling. His expression perfectly polished and pleasant.

The mask was on.

"I'm afraid I must leave. An urgent errand, but I won't be long."

"Did Malenfant send you that letter? Did they find Emile?" she blurted out.

"No, nothing to do with Emile." He took her hand and kissed it. "I swear to you, Violette, you'll be the first to know when I have news."

There was no lie, no deceit in his eyes. But there was something else. Something the mask couldn't hide completely. And it looked almost like fear.

Chapter Sixteen

THE CLOCK'S TICKING echoed through the sitting room. Violette stopped her pacing to glance at the time and sighed. Nicolas had not been gone an hour, but she was nearly going mad, waiting here alone. She stalked to the window and craned her neck to scrutinize the comings and goings in the Palais Royal. The light faded as dusk settled, but she could still make out a few people darting through the square swaddled in dark wool coats.

Where was Nicolas? When was he coming back? Lord above, if anything should happen to him…

She bit back a scream of frustration. Even if she did go out, she had no idea where he had gone. Which was certainly why he hadn't given her any information on his whereabouts—to keep her from going after him.

Blast, he knew her too well. How could he expect, then, for her to stay here with nothing to do but worry herself sick?

She ran the words he'd exchanged with Pierre in her mind. *If anyone tries to break in, you take her to the staircase immediately.* Whatever he was doing, it was connected with the Boneman, she was certain of it. The miscreant had already burned down Saint Aphrodise, but the hint of fear she'd seen in Nicolas's gaze told her this must be even worse. Or at least bad enough that he thought she might be in danger, even here.

"Madame?"

She whipped around. Pierre stood at the door, holding a small silver platter stacked with envelopes.

"A letter came for you with the afternoon post. It's at the top of the pile."

Emile. Her heart leaped… only to fall again when she realized her mistake. He couldn't possibly know she was here. Just like she had not the slightest idea where he was.

"Thank you, Pierre."

She took the letter, and he left the room. A strange pounding filled her ears as her gaze darted over the name and address scratched hastily on the envelope. It wasn't just Emile. Who could possibly know she was here?

Stupid, foolish girl. Who do you think?

With trembling fingers, she ripped the envelope open and unfolded the letter.

I have Suzanne Foucher, but it's you I want. Be at Chaillot Gate at nightfall. If you bring Lefevre or anyone else, she dies. — JL

Her legs nearly gave way. She stepped back and fell onto the couch, heart pounding so hard she was dizzy with it.

Suzanne. They had taken Suzanne. Lenoir had her.

She closed her eyes and covered her mouth. Oh God, this was why Nicolas had left so abruptly. Raoul must have sent word. And Nicolas hadn't told her, because he didn't want to alarm her, or make her feel guilty. Yes, this was far, far worse than an old church burning down. Enough to put fear in the eyes of a man like Nicolas.

Her fault. It was her fault. There was no telling what Lenoir would do to Suzanne, not to mention the Boneman and whatever horrors he could come up with.

Sweat pearled on her forehead, and she fought back a wave of nausea. It was a trap, a deadly trap, but she was well and truly caught. If she went to Chaillot, they might kill Suzanne anyway.

But if she didn't…

Find Nicolas. Warn him. She glanced out the window at the deep blue dusk. Was there even time? Besides, if she did go to him, Nicolas would never let her anywhere near Lenoir. He would sooner keep her under lock and key and take his chances to rescue Suzanne himself. But if Suzanne died…

Violette would never be able to live with herself. The guilt would eat away at her as long as she lived. She couldn't simply leave her to whatever horrid fate those villains had in store.

No, she must go. Get out of here somehow. Out the front door? No, it must be locked, and Pierre certainly had instructions not to let her leave. Would she able to fight him off? Even if she did, he would warn Nicolas as quickly as possible. If she could find a way to leave undetected… Another way out…

Take her to the staircase immediately.

Realization washed over her. Yes, of course.

Nicolas couldn't mean the main staircase. There must be a servants' staircase in the building. Several, in fact. The Palais Royal was once the residence of the king's brother, and palaces had hidden doors and corridors running parallel to the rooms. In fact, it was the first thing she'd searched for when Cransac had locked her up: a hidden door leading to the service stairs.

She stuffed the letter in her pocket and glanced around the sitting room. If there had been a hidden door there, it had long been covered with wallpaper and wainscotting. Perhaps in Nicolas's bedroom… If he needed a way to escape quickly, there was no better place for a secret exit.

She jumped to her feet and hurried to the bedroom. Her gaze ran the length of the wall, but the paneling gave nothing away. In broad daylight, perhaps…

Nightfall. You must hurry. She slid her palm along the wall, feeling for an indent. One wall… Two… *There.* The tiniest hollow between the wall and the trim. She flattened her hand against it and pushed.

Click.

It opened a crack just large enough for her to grab hold with her fingers inside and pry it open. On the other side was darkness.

She hastened to retrieve her wool shawl and shoes from her trunk. She tried not to look at the rumpled bed. For a few hours, a few days, she'd known bliss. It was more than many people could say, but the loss tore her heart to shreds. Perhaps it would have been better not to know at all what it was like to be warm and safe and cherished.

Loved.

Tears blurred her vision but she swept them away. None of it made any difference. She would not leave Suzanne to take her place, and pay for it with her life.

As soon as Violette emerged from the fiacre, she understood why Lenoir had instructed her to meet him at Chaillot Gate. Where a castle had once stood, there was nothing but an empty, sprawling square, stuck between the outer wall of Paris and the Seine. No buildings, no trees, not even a few ruins. Nothing where someone could hide and mount an attack.

She made her way to the gate through the muddy gravel and the puddles of melted snow. Another fiacre was waiting there, driver hunched in his seat, a single lantern lit. A silhouette moved in front of it, then stepped into the circle of yellow light. Brown hair, a strong jaw, broad shoulders... Her insides roiled with disgust.

"Right on time," Lenoir said. "I'm most pleased to see you, Violette. I must admit, I thought we might not meet again. Here, come closer."

By God, the mere sight of his face, the sound of his falsely courteous voice... Red-hot fury coursed through her veins, smothering her disgust to leave only anger. She forced herself to approach, one step at a time.

"Where is Suzanne?"

"In the fiacre. Don't worry, as soon as you're inside, I'll let the little harlot go."

She dug her nails in her palms. "If you hurt her in any way…"

"You'll do what? You can try to fight me, you presumptuous bitch, but I'm not a slow, lazy tub of lard like Cransac. I'll hit back tenfold."

"The Boneman told you, then."

He smirked. "Not directly. But Estienne was enraged and word gets around. Everyone knows Malenfant's men broke you out, and since Lefevre is working for him now… I figured you'd show your gratitude by spreading your legs for that bastard."

"I'm surprised you and Estienne went through all the trouble to retrieve spoiled goods," she shot back. "But it only proves you're too cowardly to attack Nicolas directly."

"Me and Estienne?" His face contorted with rage. "Estienne had nothing to do with this plan. I'm the one who put it all into place. He doesn't even know I'm here."

For a moment, shock prevented her from speaking. "What? But why?"

Lenoir grabbed her wrist and shook her. "Because I'm fucking tired of kissing his arse and still having my due taken away. You were supposed to be *mine*. *My* prize. And then Estienne sells you to Cransac. You'd have left that place no better than a broken marionette, if you'd have left at all."

If Lenoir was turning on Estienne, perhaps she could still reason with him. "Listen to me. Nicolas could help you. You were friends once, if only you—"

"Shut your mouth!" he roared, spittle flying from his lips. "Get into the fucking fiacre. By day's break, we'll be far away from this shithole."

He pulled Violette toward the door and wrenched it open. *Suzanne.* Hands tied behind her back, a gag covering her mouth, but she was there.

Her gaze met Violette's and widened. She shook her head frantically.

Lenoir pushed Violette inside, then dragged Suzanne out, flinging her to the muddy ground. Then he slammed the door shut and knocked on the ceiling. The fiacre rolled into motion. Violette grabbed the door handle. Lenoir's fingers sank into her hair and yanked her back. Pain shot through her scalp, and she cried out.

"Do not test my patience, for I have none left," Lenoir growled, keeping a tight hold on her hair.

She stared helplessly out the window. They had just passed the gate. Where was he taking her? How far would they go?

"You see, I am true to my word," he added, his tone more measured. "A fair exchange. I am not the monster you think me to be."

An empty laugh burst from her lips. "I do not think you a monster. I think you a fool. A weak, ignorant fool who has never had the spine to stand up for himself."

"Perhaps not until now. But I will take great pleasure in showing you that there is nothing weak about me."

He released her hair to wrap an arm around her waist and pulled her closer to him. Heaven help her, if she had to die fighting him off, she would.

The fiacre stopped.

Lenoir pounded against the wall. "*Allez!* What's the problem?"

The door on his side opened to Estienne's grinning skeleton face.

No. No, not that, anything but that. Dread caught in her throat, and she scrambled back into the seat.

"How nice of you to do all the dirty work for me, Jacques."

He held up his lantern and inspected Violette.

"You've been passed around quite a lot these last few days, haven't you, my dear? Unfortunately, some clients prefer stealing rather than buying fair and square."

"Estienne… Marcel… I can explain," Lenoir started. "I swear I—"

"There now, don't bother. I've known what you were planning from the start. Good a way as any to get the girl back. You have my thanks."

The blade of a knife flashed in the yellow glow. And plunged straight into Lenoir's chest. He drew a horrible, gurgling breath as blood seeped out onto his shirt.

Violette screamed.

"Shame I had to put him down," Estienne said, almost conversationally. "But I think I can find one last use for him."

He retrieved his knife, and a fresh spurt of blood gushed forth. Violette kept her eyes fixed on the blade, and wondered if she was next.

Chapter Seventeen

"WHO TOOK HER? They paid you to hand over Suzanne, didn't they? You better fucking answer me!"

Nicolas grabbed Raoul's upper arm to hold him back. His friend leaned over Lili Foucher, who sat on a tatty velvet divan, her pudgy face fixed in a sullen pout. So far, she'd remained tight-lipped under their questioning, only admitting that Suzanne had dropped by the Sirène that morning at her behest.

"I already told you, I don't know nothing," she muttered.

"So she vanished into thin air, then?" Raoul growled, pulling against Nicolas's arm. Goddamn it, it was like trying to hold back a rabid bear. "What kind of fucking idiot do you take me for? If you'd were a man, I'd have you spitting out your rotten teeth!"

By God, he was tempted to let Raoul give in to his anger, but that would get them nowhere. After all, the main reason he'd come with Raoul was to make sure his friend didn't burn down the entire brothel in a fit of rage.

"There, my friend. No need for violence. Suzanne will do the honors herself when we get her back. You wouldn't want to deprive her of that pleasure, would you?"

"Fuck you!"

Raoul wrenched free and turned away, prowling to the back of the small salon.

Nicolas crossed his arms over his chest. It took all his energy to remain calm and not throttle answers out of that woman.

"Try harder," he snapped. "Your profits wouldn't be nearly as much if Malenfant decided to take a larger commission."

Because every brothel in this city belonged to either Malenfant or the Boneman, and brought their respective organizations innumerable francs.

She scowled. "What the bloody hell are you talking about?"

"Anyone who paid you to turn Suzanne over to them is working for the Boneman. Trust me, you'd rather deal with me than tell Malenfant directly. Better pray the time you're costing us won't have dire consequences for everyone involved."

Lili snorted, but her dull brown eyes sharpened with fear. "Fine. It was a man with brown hair. Handsome, tall, well built."

He frowned. "Go on."

"He talked like a gentleman. Paid in full, too."

Lenoir. It had to be him. Running another one of the Boneman's grisly errands.

"I didn't take him for a thug," she added, as if that excused her actions. "I thought he was just another one of Suzanne's lovers."

Raoul pounded his fist against the wall, and Lili jumped in her seat. Blast, Nicolas was going to have to get him out of here before he demolished something.

"Did he come alone?"

"Yes."

Raoul glared at her over his shoulder. "You're lying. I've seen Suzanne fight off men twice her size. She wouldn't have let anyone carry her off like that."

Lili looked sideways, her expression shuttered once again. Tapping her foot. Nicolas tightened his fists.

"You gave her something to drink, didn't you? Drugged her wine?"

She pressed her lips together, her eyes hardening. Devil take it, they were wasting precious time with the wench. Either way, the result was the same.

He buttoned his coat. "Charming. But we have no time to deal with you now. Come, Raoul, let us go."

Raoul shot Lili a murderous look, but reluctantly pushed himself away from the wall, leaving a fist-sized crater in the plaster.

Outside the brothel, the street lanterns glowed, but their light seemed feeble and fleeting against the winter gloom. A quiver of panic rippled in Nicolas's gut. Blast, that interrogation had taken longer than he'd expected. Longer than necessary. He must get back to Violette soon... but then what to do about Suzanne? He couldn't simply leave Raoul to search by himself while he sat waiting for Estienne to send a ransom note.

For Estienne would undoubtedly demand a trade. Violette for Suzanne. The worst possible exchange he could imagine.

Raoul stalked toward Capucine Boulevard. "Damn that whore. This has gotten us nowhere."

Nicolas lengthened his stride to catch up. "At least now we're certain Suzanne must be in one of the Boneman's haunts. If Talloche got my message, reinforcements should be here soon."

"By God, if only I'd gone with her... Yesterday, I told her..." His voice caught, and he paused for a moment. "I told her I was worried for her safety, but she simply laughed, said she could handle herself... You know how she is."

Yes. Nicolas did know. But he couldn't reply. Raoul's words struck too close to the knot of fear that was building in his chest. His pace quickened. He needed to get home, make sure Violette was safe.

They walked the rest of the way in silence. When they turned toward the barbershop, Nicolas spotted a silhouette pacing in front of the door. Someone was waiting for them. He squinted.

Pierre.

His breath froze in his chest, blood turning to liquid ice in his veins. If Pierre was here...

"What are you doing here?" He broke into a jog. "Where is

Violette?"

Pierre's eyes were wide with shock, watery with fear. "*Monsieur*, she... She's gone. Left the apartment. I don't—"

A black torrent of rage swirled up in an instant, drowning all reason or restraint. He grabbed Pierre by the shoulders and shook him. "*She's gone?* How the bloody hell is that possible? Did you just let her walk out, damn you?"

Raoul grabbed his shoulder, pulled him back. "For fuck's sake, Nicolas, don't kill the man before he explains."

Yes. Yes, Raoul was right. Listen first, then decide whether he should break every one of Pierre's limbs, bone by bone. Raoul unlocked the door and ushered them inside.

"I'll stand guard out front," he told Nicolas. "You take him to the back room."

Nicolas nodded. Pierre followed him through the front of the shop.

Nicolas flung his hat onto the table. "Sit. You have ten seconds to explain."

Shoulders trembling, Pierre sank into the seat. "She found the hidden staircase, *monsieur*. I swear I didn't hear anything. I ran here as soon as I noticed she was gone."

Nicolas curled his fingers around the back of a chair, grip tightening until his palms burned. "No sign of damage?"

"No, the door was intact, opened from the inside. One moment, I left *Mademoiselle* to read the post, and when I came back to ask what she wanted for dinner, not half an hour later..."

"Wait a moment." He leaned over the table. "The post? Someone sent her a letter?"

Pierre swallowed and nodded shakily. "I... I thought you might have sent word of her whereabouts to her family and..."

Nicolas rubbed his hands over his face. Pierre was ever a dutiful servant. Never peeking at the messages Nicolas sent out, always minding his own business. Nicolas hadn't divulged the gritty details of Violette's situation, and Pierre hadn't asked. How could he possibly guess that a simple letter might be as deadly as a bottle of poison?

"You stupid whoreson," he growled.

But he wasn't talking to Pierre. He was talking to himself. He was so anxious to keep Violette safe and protected, so certain that Estienne would either contact him first offering this impossible trade or attack with brute force, that he'd been blind to any other possibility.

He should have known better. Estienne never did the expected. No, he favored the crueler, more unusual path. Creeping in the darkness from the smallest of cracks instead of forcing a door open. The guilt Violette must have felt learning that Suzanne was missing… Small wonder she'd sneaked out.

"I… I looked, but I couldn't find the letter anywhere and I knew I must warn you as quickly as possible," Pierre said. "Perhaps if I conducted a more thorough search…"

She must have taken it. She didn't want to leave a trail. The instructions must have been clear.

Think. Think, damn you. Fix your mistake.

Nicolas raked his hand through his hair. "Right, I suppose there's not much else you can do. Try to find that letter and hold the fort while I'm gone."

He needed to get his hands on Lenoir. Yes, Lenoir would be easier to catch, and if he already knew where Suzanne was…

The crash of shattering glass echoed from the front room. Nicolas reached into his pocket and whipped out his knife.

"Bloody fucking hell!" Raoul bellowed from the other side of the door.

Nicolas wrenched it open. Raoul crouched next to a box, shards of glass scattered at his feet, his face entirely drained of blood. Greenish, as if he was about to be sick.

Strands of matted brown hair peeked out from the open top.

"Lenoir," Raoul managed.

Nicolas took careful steps toward the box. Looked. And felt nothing.

All thoughts, all feelings fled from his mind, retreating to the dark room that had formed the day he'd stood amid the crowd at the Concorde, watching his brother and father dragged to the guillotine. The swish of a silver blade, a torrent of blood, the executioner brandishing the head by the hair to savage cheers…

He must lock the room. Keep everything there. If he didn't, his confrontation with Estienne would end in disaster, just as it had before.

He stared down at the mangled head. No note. Just letters carved into the cold flesh of the forehead.

E-N-F-E-R.

Hell. Where Estienne was waiting for him.

ROUGH HANDS DRAGGED Violette down a flight of stony steps. A foul, musty smell invaded her nostrils. Down and down they went, and the air closed in around her. Panic clenched her throat.

Estienne's men had blindfolded her and bound her hands the moment she descended from the fiacre. They'd made her walk, then tossed her into another fiacre, and finally brought her here. Probably still in Paris, or just on the outskirts, as it had not taken very long to reach their destination.

Violette nearly tripped. The stairs had given way to a flat surface. Her captor wordlessly held her up by the elbow and shoved her forward.

A burnt smell now. Torches. Men's voices echoing in the distance. And the atmosphere strangely warm, almost hot. She kept walking. *Just one more step. Just one more step.*

"Stop. Sit here."

She held out her tied hands for balance and slowly lowered herself to the dusty ground.

"Don't move."

The footsteps moved away, and she was left alone. Minutes ticked by, or maybe hours. Her limbs were numb, her muscles stiff, her wrists chaffed by the rope. Would she simply be left here to die?

Footsteps again. Different. Lighter. Fingers loosened the knot of her blindfold, and it fell around her neck.

The Boneman loomed over her. "Welcome to my humble abode."

Her gaze darted to and fro.

Bones. Bones everywhere. Piles of them as high as the wall, yellowed with age and the light of the torches. The skulls' empty sockets stared back at her, but they were far less frightening than the man who hovered above her.

"Don't worry, my dear, you won't be here long. You're just bait to catch a bigger fish."

Nicolas. It was Nicolas he wanted. Hope and dread warred within her, tearing at her gut and leaving a sheen of cold sweat on her skin. Hope that he would come, and dread because that was the Boneman's plan.

"As soon as that's done, I'll have you moved to a brothel in some piss-soaked back alley. You won't find it much more enjoyable than servicing Cransac, but as my whore of a mother used to say, you made your bed, now lie it in. Literally."

A dreadful smile stretched his lips, as if he'd just made a pleasant joke.

"Nicolas will kill you," she spat. "You'll be left here to rot with the other corpses."

His grin widened over his large teeth. "Oh, he tried once, did he tell you that? It didn't quite work out the way he'd planned."

A man emerged from the dark corridor that led into the room. "Lefevre is here."

"Splendid. Bring him in." He took his knife from his pocket, snapping it open, and seized Violette's arm to haul her to her feet. "Let us see if he thinks twice before making the same mistake again."

Chapter Eighteen

THE SQUARE AROUND the Barrière d'Enfer was pitch black under the cloudy night sky, but Nicolas's footsteps remained steady and determined as he crossed toward the entrance to the catacombs.

As a member of the same gang as Lenoir and Estienne, he'd been down there many times. The catacombs had once been quarries and had lain abandoned for years, a boon for smugglers, a discreet way to travel from one neighborhood to another undetected—if you knew your way around the sprawling maze of galleries carved in the stone. And if you didn't, you'd be lost forever in the dark.

The place had always fascinated Estienne. He'd wanted to turn the left bank's network of tunnels into his empire, and in a sense he had. His headquarters lay above an opening to the north, and he controlled the southernmost entrance at the Barrière d'Enfer, as well.

Which was why he wanted Nicolas here. Once inside the catacombs, it was much harder to get out.

Two thugs waited by the entrance. They uncovered their lantern to look Nicolas over.

"Nicolas Lefevre," he said. "Your master's waiting for me."

One of them spit out a wad of tobacco and put his hand to the pistol stuck in his belt. "Spread your arms."

Nicolas retrieved his knife from his pocket and handed it over. "Here, I'll save you the trouble."

"Still have to do it. A man can have more than one knife."

Nicolas extended his arms, and the man patted him down. He wasn't surprised, or distressed, or worried. *Nothing.* Nothing left in his mind but intense, moment-by-moment concentration on the job at hand.

"Come on."

The man took the lantern and led him down stone steps. They made their way through a winding, torch-lit gallery, past a cove where other men were opening crates and examining their contents. They continued between the piles of bones lining the walls.

None of it scared Nicolas. A skull was far less shocking than a severed head, and bones were just bones. The dead didn't kill or injure or rape. Only the living could.

The man stopped and nodded him forward. "Through here."

Nicolas entered a large room. A surge of nausea ripped through his stomach. Before him, stood his worst nightmare come to life.

Estienne held Violette against him, one arm wrapped around her waist. Her wrists were tied. He held a long, thin blade at his side. Grinning like a ghoul.

The same way he'd held Laurine. The same knife. Dragging Nicolas back to that night a decade ago, in a ramshackle room in one of the tenements of Palais Royal. He'd tried to defend Laurine, tried to convince Lenoir he shouldn't, *couldn't* let Estienne have her just because he was the leader of their gang. Lenoir was supposed to protect his girl, not hand her over in an absurd display of loyalty.

Have mercy, I beg of you. Please, Jacques... Nicolas... Don't let him do this...

He'd challenged Estienne to a fight. And Estienne had beaten him bloody before ordering the other boys to tie him up.

Nicolas froze. Then Violette's gaze met his—pale as frost, brimming with fear, but something else shone there as well. Something soft and deep that reached inside his chest and wrenched at his heart.

Emotion came rushing back to him like a tidal wave. Horror and rage and disgust. And a fierce, furious love for the woman standing a few meters from him, so strong that it ignited the darkness within to a blazing inferno.

It pulled him back to the present. He wasn't the helpless boy he'd been in that room, bruised and bound and forced to watch as the Boneman raped Laurine again and again. He was stronger, and he burned with more than the simple need for justice and vengeance.

Violette had done this to him. Mended the gaping wound he'd tried to ignore for years, and made him complete.

She had to live. This was the only thing that mattered. *She had to live.*

Energy jolted through his body with the need to smash and tear and crush. No matter if that whoreson was armed. No matter if he himself would die. He would take Estienne down with him, and Violette would be free.

"So kind of you to accept my invitation," Estienne said. "How long has it been, Lefevre?"

He lifted his chin and crossed his arms. "Not long enough. And it'll be a very short reunion."

"Why, you're hurting my feelings, old friend."

Estienne raised the blade to Violette's jugular. Every hair on Nicolas's body stood on end, his nerves on alert. *He won't kill her now. He's using her as bait. He needs something from you.*

"I thought you might want to reminisce. Talk about the good times we had when we were boys."

He shook his head. "Haven't you heard, Marcel? This is a new century. The past is over and done with. Soon no one will remember your misdeeds or even your name. You'll be nothing more than another pile of bones."

Estienne's smile vanished, and his gaze hardened. Cold, black, ruthless. He pressed the blade harder, drawing a pearl of blood, and Violette's mouth parted in a whimper.

For a fleeting moment, Nicolas locked eyes with her. *I'm here. We'll find a way.*

"You should do well to remember the past, old friend. You forgot the lesson I taught you last time we met and look where you are now." Estienne sighed. "I shall simply have to teach you again."

Nicolas's limbs shook with contained fury. *Not now. Wait. Think.*

"It seems using Lenoir's girl wasn't effective in teaching you your place," he added. "Perhaps if I get between this little bitch's legs, you'll finally learn to heel."

Violette squeezed her eyes shut. "Please don't hurt me," she nearly sobbed. "I'll do whatever you want."

"There now, I just want to have a bit of fun, that's all. And make sure Lefevre can behave himself. You're like a pretty little leash for my new dog."

A strangled cry emerged from her throat, and she slumped against Estienne, as if losing consciousness. Estienne snickered with glee.

"*Aristo* girls. Doesn't take much to make them swoon, does it? Bah, a few weeks in a brothel, and she'll—"

A violent jerk of her head and Violette's skull met Estienne's nose with a loud crack. His words died on a yowl, and his hold on her slackened. She rolled to the ground.

Nicolas launched himself at Estienne. "Stay back!" he shouted to Violette, who scrambled away as she best she could with her hands tied.

Estienne clamped his hand over his nose, blood gushing between his fingers, but his gaze immediately focused on Nicolas. He whipped his blade in front of him and released his nose to reveal the bottom half of his face slick and red.

"I'll gut you like a fucking pig." He slashed his blade again.

"I'll gouge your fucking eyes out and shove them down that whore's throat."

Devil take it, he was fast. Faster than Nicolas remembered. And the length of his arms increased his reach. Nicolas couldn't even get close enough for a proper kick without risking a cut to the chest.

Slash.

Nicolas stepped back, again, again. Losing ground, unable to attack.

Think. Use it to your advantage.

He curled in on himself and bent his arms into a shield. Estienne grinned. The bastard knew he was winning.

Or thought so, at least. Nicolas's legs hit a pile of bones, and he fell back. Estienne lunged at him. His fingers curled around the first thing they touched and pulled. A bone. He swung it. Hard. Right into Estienne's temple.

Crack.

Estienne roared in pain and dropped his knife. *Now.* Nicolas jumped to his feet and rammed his fists into Estienne's gut.

Knuckles slammed into his jaw. Pain exploded in front of his eyes. The merciless punch of someone who had fought to the death in the streets.

He didn't let up. Couldn't. *Violette.* He couldn't fail her. Chest, ribs, a kick to the gut, one to the knee. Estienne lurched back, but the bastard's reach was too bloody long. One foot planted, and he sprang once more on the attack…

Estienne's hands wrapped around Nicolas's neck, his long fingers wringing his windpipe like an iron vise. He gasped for air, but none came, and a flood of alarm engulfed him. Black spots threatened his vision. From the corner of his eye, movement. *Violette.* Staggering to her feet.

A flash of silver on the ground.

Of course.

He let his entire body slacken and crumple.

Estienne squeezed tighter, mouth twisted in a vicious smile.

"See you in hell, old friend."

Nicolas turned his head. Violette kicked the knife in his direction, and it skidded across the ground. Estienne released his grip, and his weight crushed Nicolas as he grabbed for the weapon. But Nicolas's arm was already outstretched.

His fingers curled about the handle, grip sure, and he thrust the blade upward. It sunk into flesh and muscle and bone. Plunged in to the hilt. A stream of hot blood soaked his shirt. Estienne's chest rattled in a dreadful gurgle, and his body slumped forward.

Nicolas heaved the lifeless body away and it rolled into the pile of bones. Estienne's empty eyes stared up at the stone ceiling.

"You first, old friend," he panted, then worked the knife loose before rushing to Violette.

VIOLETTE STUMBLED TOWARD Nicolas. His breathing came in harsh puffs. A bloody welt stood out on his cheekbone, a large crimson stain on his chest—but not his, thank God. He was alive. *Alive*, while the Boneman lay dead. Tears sprang to her eyes and rolled down her cheeks.

He reached for her forearm and sawed at the rope until it fell away, freeing her wrists. She wrapped her arms around him. Solid and warm and *there*. By God, she would never let him go again.

He stroked her hair soothingly and kissed the top of her head. "I'm here. All is well, my love. It's over now. All is well."

Reality struck her again. The Boneman might be dead, but they were still stuck in his lair. "His men… They'll come after us. They must have heard."

"Undoubtedly. But I warrant the Boneman told them not to intervene. It would have shown weakness to ask for help in fighting one man." He smiled. "He didn't count on fighting a second opponent though."

"But how will we get out?"

"Don't worry, this isn't my first time in the catacombs. I know other ways out."

He took her hand and grabbed one of the torches on the wall, then nodded toward a dark, narrow tunnel leading out of the room. Pure instinct nailed her feet to the ground.

"Nicolas… If we get lost…"

"We won't." He squeezed her hand. "Do you trust me?"

Of course. She trusted him with her life, several times over. She nodded, and they started off.

The tunnel twisted on and on. Nicolas never hesitated, only stopping a few times to read strange inscriptions carved into the walls by torchlight before continuing. He never let go of her, and Violette only focused on the warmth of his palm against hers, the sureness of his step.

He had pulled her out of the darkness before. He would do it again.

But she was tired, so very tired. The path beneath their trudging feet had been running somewhat upward for what felt like an eternity. How long would the torch last? What if it started to peter out?

"We're almost there," he said, as if reading her thoughts. "Just around this corner…"

Indeed, the gallery turned a sharp left. Up ahead, a square of blue. Relief overwhelmed her with such force that her legs nearly gave out.

"You go first, love," Nicolas said, and led her to a small stone ledge.

She stepped onto it and hoisted herself through the opening into a muddy alley. Nicolas was right behind her. He threw the torch on the wet ground and took off his coat to drape it over her shoulders.

"Ah, I never thought I'd be so glad to be cold," he sighed.

"Where are we?"

He nodded toward the spire of a church that peeked over the

rooftops. "Behind Saint-Germain-des-Près. Come along."

They walked through the winding streets. The sky was turning a paler shade of blue. They passed by shop keepers and laborers and craftsmen who barely spared a glance at their grimy attire, arriving at the banks of the Seine just as the sun rose.

Nicolas's arm wrapped around her waist, and he held her tightly. "See? The Palais Royal is just across the river. We'll be home soon."

The sunlight rippled on the gray water. And for the first time, she saw just how beautiful it was.

Chapter Nineteen

V IOLETTE WOKE TO an empty bed.

She stretched on the soft sheets. Where was Nicolas? How long had she been asleep? A ray of waning sunlight shone through the gap in the curtains.

Pierre was waiting when they got home with word from Raoul that Suzanne had reappeared safe and sound. The same wave of relief Violette had experienced on escaping the catacombs overwhelmed her once more, but it seemed to drain all her energy.

Nicolas had immediately ordered a hot bath, and she'd dozed off in the hot water, only to awaken to the soft strokes of a towel drying her. Nicolas had gone on to pull her nightrail over her head, before carrying her to bed where she'd sunk into slumber again.

At some point, she'd emerged from sleep to find his arms around her, cradling her against him, then sank once more into oblivion.

Now she was well and truly awake. She flung back the covers and padded into the sitting room. Empty as well, but the door yawned into the corridor.

"Nicolas?" she called.

Footsteps echoing on the hardwood floor announced his

arrival. "Ah, you're awake. Wonderful. I returned not five minutes ago."

"You went out?"

"Only to go see Raoul and Suzanne."

She rushed to him and took his hands. "How is she? Is she hurt?"

"Just a gash on her forehead, but otherwise, she's fine. And I have more good news." He closed the door behind him and pulled her to the divan. "They found Emile."

Violette's heart stopped in her chest. *Emile.* Emile was alive. "Thank the heavens."

"Malenfant's men had been fishing for information in exchange for a few francs around the Grands Boulevards. Someone approached them, saying Emile had been hiding at his place. Word is getting around that Estienne is dead, so I suppose Emile's friend thought it was safe." Nicolas frowned. "Apparently, while he was hiding, he asked this friend of his to lock him in a room and wean him off of drink."

Violette gasped. "What?"

"The friend agreed. It was very foolish. Emile could have died. But he got through it."

Her brother wanted a fresh start, then. Just like she did. She pressed her hand against her heart, beating quickly now, with hope and apprehension. Nicolas studied her, his green eyes soft and serious.

"If you wish to return home… After all, you and your brother were living there for quite some time."

Violette shook her head. "It was never a happy place for us. We could sell it, or rent it. But not live in it, not anymore."

Too many ugly memories. And even with carpets and a roaring hearth, it would always be a cold place for her.

"Emile and I are both old enough to lead our own lives. I… I need to figure out what I'm good at, if anything. I was never really given the chance to ask myself this question."

Nicolas brushed a strand of hair and tucked it behind her ear.

"I am certain you possess a myriad of talents, my love. And it will be my pleasure to help you discover them."

"And…" She sidled closer to him. "I want to stay. With you. If you want the same…"

"Of course, I do," he interrupted her. "How could you doubt it?"

"I care little what people will say, if they call me your mistress…"

"My mistress!" He shook his head. "Not my mistress, Violette. Damn it, woman, you pick pockets, you break out of houses, and you manage to trick the most dangerous man in Paris in the face of mortal danger. You'll be at my side as an equal, Violette, nothing less. And I will marry you as such. I love you."

"Nicolas…"

She flung herself into his arms. No words had given her more joy in all her life, and they shone bright and true, filling her with light.

"I love you too. So very much. I never wish to be parted from you."

"Good." He pushed her shoulders back to kiss her once, twice, three times, each kiss lingering longer on her lips. "I have no further plans to go out today. One hour away from you is quite enough."

He pulled her closer, and their mouths met again. Hunger stirred within her—hunger for him. Her body craved his touch like it did water, food, sunlight. An irresistible necessity that demanded its due.

She moaned as his tongue stroked hers languidly, grasping his wrist to bring his hand to her thigh, then up to her breast, already heavy with want. He squeezed, and delicious heat gathered at the tip.

"My, I feared you might be too tired for my attentions," he murmured wickedly. "I'm exceedingly pleased to be proven wrong once again."

"Nicolas," she groaned. "Take me to bed, I beg of you."

"Right away? I think we can put the divan to good use first."

He knelt on the floor in front of her and bunched her nightrail up her legs. Up and up and up. Revealing her entirely to him.

Violette squirmed and arched her back. His gaze alone sent curls of fire through her belly. "Nicolas… What are you doing?"

"Giving you pleasure, my love. As much as I possibly can." He leaned down, and his mouth grazed her thigh. "I promise you'll like this."

He planted small kisses on her skin and delicately spread her legs. Up and up and… *Oh*. His mouth, it was… On her. Completely. His tongue flicked, and…

"*Oh*, oh Lord, what…"

The sensation was indescribable. Too exquisite for words. Every time he flicked and licked and, *heavens*, he was sucking lightly now, and each one of her breaths turned into a little cry.

"Nicolas," she mewled. "Don't… don't stop, I…"

"Never," he panted against her. "You taste too damn good for me to stop."

He sucked harder now, and almost unbearable pleasure swept through her in wave after wave, in time with the greedy pulls of his mouth, bringing her higher, higher still, until she was dizzy with it and words spilled out of her mouth of their own accord. *More, please, more*, she was so close, so…

His tongue swirled at her entrance, and her hips jerked, welcoming its invasion, her muscles clenching as if to draw it in while she rode the crest of her pleasure.

Too much. It was too much. She opened her eyes, lungs working to catch her breath.

"I told you you'd like it," Nicolas teased.

Lord, his lips… They were slick with her essence, and he passed his tongue over them so as not to lose a single drop.

"I did. Very much."

He rose to his feet and took her hand, then hooked his arm under her legs and carried her to the bedroom.

Moments later, she lay on the mattress, watching him undress—no, tear off his clothes, more like, and dropping them in heaps to the floor. He unbuttoned his waistcoat with such haste a button popped.

He felt the same urgency she did. The same uncontrollable yearning. They'd come so close to losing each other forever…

No, that was over and done with. He was here. They were here, together, and nothing could separate them again.

"Nicolas," she breathed. "I need you inside me."

"I won't keep you waiting, love." He stretched on the bed but remained on his back instead of positioning himself over her, slowly stroking his hardened manhood. "Straddle me. Much as you did on the chair that first night. I want to watch you."

She carefully placed her legs on either side of him and pressed her throbbing nub against his erection, seeking the delectable pressure she now knew so well. Her slick folds slid over his length, and he closed his eyes in a groan.

"Yes, start like that if you wish… By God, that's good. You're so beautiful, giving yourself pleasure on my cock."

She rolled her hips, drowning in the sensation of the slippery friction between them. Nicolas gripped her waist and halted her movements.

"Stop there, love, or I'll come. Take me inside you now."

She hovered over him, delicately handling his manhood at her entrance, then slowly lowered herself. The way he stretched her, filled her so completely… She gave in to the sensation, and he thrust his hips upwards, burying himself to the hilt in her sheath. For moment, she couldn't think, couldn't breathe. She could only feel.

Then she moved, and the feeling came to life, little bursts of heat in her body that gathered in her center, more and more of them, coming together to merge in an uncontrollable fire.

"Keep going," she pleaded.

"You're the one who's moving," he laughed. "I'm hardly doing anything at all."

"I… I wish to feel you deeper."

He groaned and kneaded the soft flesh of her thighs before tightening his hold on her. "Do you? Hard and fast, then?"

He met the sway of her hips with powerful thrusts, each one sharper than the last, and she arched her back to welcome them.

"*Yes*, oh goodness, just like that. *More.*"

"Fucking hell," Nicolas cursed, and increased the vigor of his movements. "Harder?"

"Please, yes, *anything*, I'm so close…"

His fingers dug into her thigh, so roughly she was sure they would leave a bruise. She didn't care. She wanted him, all of him, as much as he could give her. The tip of his manhood hit a spot so deep that it brought her out of herself, out of her body, *oh God, oh God*, she would die from the force of it. Her muscles clenched, released, over and over, until her body gave a great shudder, and she floated back down.

Nicolas jerked his hips, then lifted her to spill his seed on his belly. She slumped onto the bed next to him. Somehow, the pale trickles of wetness on his skin made her feel a twinge of loss. How good it would feel if he didn't pull back, if he stayed inside her even at the moment of his abandon…

Later. It would come later. There was no hurry now. She curled against him and nuzzled his shoulder. His breathing calmed, grew deeper.

"Don't be cross if I doze off," he mumbled. "I will be ready and eager to go again after a proper rest."

"Sleep, my love." She kissed his skin. "We have all the time in the world."

NICOLAS SLAPPED HIS hand on the polished counter of the Cabaret Doré. "Champagne for all of us! Your very finest, if you please."

Suzanne dropped into a mock curtsy. "Right away, *monsieur.*

I'll see what we have in the cellar."

She disappeared down a small hatch behind the counter. Violette leaned over and craned her neck to see where it led. Nicolas breathed a whiff of lavender and soap and *her*. Lord, he would never tire of this woman's delicious scent.

"Those steps are so steep and narrow," she said. "How does she manage without falling?"

Raoul put down his pint and licked foam from his lips. "She never loses her balance. She can walk a ledge no larger than your hand. I've seen her do it. Ought to be in a circus with those skills."

Though his friend's tone was light, he had barely taken his eyes off Suzanne since their arrival, and now that she was out of sight, he tapped his fingers nervously on the counter. As if he was afraid she might vanish again.

Nicolas understood all too well. Every time he left the house, his mind returned to the night of Violette's disappearance. But he couldn't ask poor Pierre to stand guard at the hidden door, and Violette wouldn't allow it anyway. After all, she was free to come and go as she pleased now. And little by little, it would get easier.

He wouldn't protect her by locking her up. Simply by loving her. He took her hand to kiss it, and she beamed at him.

Suzanne returned with a bottle. Veuve Clicquot, no less. She pressed her thumb against the cork, and it went off with a joyous pop, flying in an arc before landing on the floor. She swiftly poured the bubbling drink into four tall glasses before handing them out. Nicolas raised his, clinking it with Violette's, then Raoul's, and finally Suzanne's.

"*Santé*, my friends. To the start of a new era of health and happiness."

Suzanne grinned. "January 1st was two weeks ago, but I'll allow it since you're paying for a very expensive bottle."

Violette smiled. "I was always told that you have until January 31st to present New Year's wishes."

"Finally, someone who knows the rules of true *savoir-vivre*,"

Suzanne said with a wink. "You'll make a lady out of me yet."

Raoul elbowed Nicolas and frowned. "Look who it is."

Nicolas turned. Malenfant and Talloche threaded their way between occupied tables. Talloche fit right in with his burn scar, but Malenfant's flashy gold pin drew more than a few stares.

"What the devil is he doing here?" Suzanne asked.

"I invited him," Nicolas replied cheerfully. "Glad he could make it."

Raoul snorted. "Have you lost your mind, man?"

Violette laid a hand on his chest. "Nicolas thought that it would make a statement to invite him onto our territory in order to… negotiate. And I agree."

Suzanne took a swig of champagne. "Say no more. As long as he ran his idea by you first and obtained your approval, I know it's not just another one of his hare-brained schemes."

Nicolas sighed. This promised to be years of fun.

Malenfant ambled up, thumbs hooked in the pockets of his waistcoat. "Good evening. So nice of you to extend an invitation. This sort of place brings me back to my youth." He patted his stomach. "I was in better fighting shape back then, but my pockets were far emptier. What are we drinking?"

Nicolas smiled. "Suzanne, can you pour two more glasses for our guests?"

Malenfant chortled. "Guests? I seem to recall the owner of this fine establishment pays his dues to me."

"Nonetheless, tonight you are my guests." He raised his glass to his lips. "I'm paying for the champagne, after all."

Malenfant observed him with a calculating gaze. "Tell me why you asked me here."

Straight to the point, then. Nicolas had expected no less. "I wish to revise the terms of our agreement. I hear that many of the Boneman's former employees have offered you their services. That must represent quite an increase in your revenue. And since I was the one to do away with your rival, I would say that I have returned your favors tenfold."

"He's not wrong there," Talloche grunted with a half-smile.

"When I'll want your opinion, I'll ask for it," Malenfant snapped, but he seemed to be mulling the question over in his head. "It is not easy to give up the sort of talent you have, Lefevre."

Nicolas lifted his chin. "Paris is yours now. You can do as you please with your newfound power, so long as you let me and my friends live our lives in peace."

"Is that a threat?"

"I watched Nicolas take down the Boneman unarmed," Violette said. "If it were a threat, believe me, he would not bother with champagne and pleasant manners."

Malenfant smiled. "The infamous Mademoiselle de la Roque. We meet at last. I can see why Lefevre raised hell to get you back." He took a champagne glass from the counter. "Very well, then. You stay out of my business and I'll stay out of yours."

Nicolas clinked his glass with his. "Splendid. *Santé, monsieur.*"

He turned back to Violette and murmured in her ear. "I rather like how well you play the role of my right-hand man. Or rather right-hand woman. Suzanne says you'll turn her into a lady, but *sacredieu*, I think you'll soon turn into a delinquent if I'm not careful."

"Really? But you haven't even finished teaching me *savate* yet."

He laughed. "All right, then. Classes resume tonight when we get home. I'm warning you, I won't relent until you're utterly exhausted."

She kissed him. She tasted like champagne and sweetness. Like *life*.

"I'll do my very best, my love."

Epilogue

Domaine d'Orgeval, April 1808

VIOLETTE INHALED THE fragrance of grass, fresh and sharp after a light rain. Now only small clouds dotted the sky, and the noonday sun shone bright. She loosened her shawl to savor its heat on her skin.

"And this is where we'll start building the new stables next month," Emile pointed toward an enclosure where three horses grazed, their bay coats glossy in the sunlight. "A considerable investment, but a very sound plan in the long run."

Violette smiled. "You seemed to have discussed the matter thoroughly with your employer."

"Indeed. Only last week, Monsieur de Cazal acquired two new studs, and already he's receiving requests for service. If his business keeps growing, the new stables will not only be necessary, but a selling point. We've been looking at the latest innovations in that area…"

She let him chatter on as they set off up the hill back to the house. Her brother's words were as soothing and comforting as the warmth of spring. She never tired of hearing him talk about his work as Guy de Cazal's steward, a position Nicolas had encouraged him to apply for five years earlier, almost to the day.

Five years. A lifetime, really. It was hard to believe the man striding next to her, speaking animatedly about efficient ventilation, his hair neatly trimmed and his hands calloused from hard work, was the same who had spent his nights drinking and his days in filth and darkness.

Every time they met, the difference struck her with greater force, and by God, it was almost enough to bring tears to her eyes.

He paused and raised an eyebrow. "What is it, sister? You look as though all this talk of transoms and awnings is making you sentimental."

She slapped his chest with the back of her hand. "It's you, you fool. It is a great joy for me to see what a splendid job you're doing." She bit back the wave of emotion rising up her throat to go on. "I'm so very proud of all you've accomplished."

He nodded and returned her smile. It took him a moment to reply. "I feel I have never managed to thank you properly. Or Nicolas either."

"Knowing you are thriving here is all the thanks we need."

"It's more than a position for me," he insisted. "Monsieur de Cazal is not only a fair employer and a good man, he understood where I was coming from, to what depths I had sunk before trying to piece my life back together."

"And you succeeded, brother. Most admirably."

She leaned over to kiss his cheek. Emile offered her his arm and they strolled along the patches of daffodils, azaleas, and hyacinths that lined the path.

"Such a beautiful day," she sighed. "I know you must get back to work, but I'll have you know Leon has been begging us to play with his dear uncle."

Emile grinned. "I'll take him fishing early tomorrow morning, how's that?"

"Perfect. Oh look, there they are."

The De Cazals' house, an elegant mansion with graceful lines and leafy friezes sculpted in the pale yellow stone, had come into view. On the lawn, guests had gathered while children darted among the assembly. In the distance, Nicolas waved his hands in shooing movements in the direction of his son, a clear attempt to convince him to join the other boys in their running and shouting. Leon, however, stuck close to his papa, fairly clinging to his leg.

Violette shook her head. "Dear me, I had better hurry and see what's wrong."

"Go on," Emile replied. "I never cease to admire what an attentive mama you are."

"Nicolas sometimes tells me I coddle Leon too much," she said with a sigh. "Perhaps he's right. I should worry less."

"That's the way you are, sister." He took her hand and squeezed it. "Protective. Kind. And we are all the better for it."

✦⟫⟫⟫❈⟪⟪⟪✦

"COME NOW, LEON, don't they look like they're having fun? Don't be afraid, Papa is right behind you."

Leon sniffled, and his tiny hand grasped the sage green wool of Nicolas's breeches.

"Samuel is your age," he continued, pointing out Guy's youngest son. "Three years old, just like you. I'm sure he'd love a friend to play with."

Leon stuck out his lower lip furiously. "No! Not my friend!"

Strong brows, just like his mama. And a strong temper as well. Nicolas patted the boy's dark hair, while Guy approached with a smile.

"No luck?"

"None so far. I have met men in the ring who outweighed me by ten kilos who were less difficult to bring to heel than this little terror."

Guy slapped his shoulder. "I wish I could tell you it'll get better, old chap, but I can only offer my sympathies."

His three boys were now tumbling in the grass, the two youngest banding together against the eldest, who stumbled straight into a doll's tea party that Jerome and Stella's daughter Clara had daintily laid out on a white tablecloth.

Her nanny sprung to her feet, dropped her knitting and stalked over to the boys, fists planted on her hips. "That's quite enough now! If you want to fight, go over by the willow tree where you won't bother anyone!"

The three boys nodded sheepishly and ran off.

"What a wonderful woman, that Jane," Guy said. "Since Stella and Jerome got here, both my throat and my nerves are ever so rested."

"Remarkable," Nicolas agreed. "Antonia told me you were searching for a new governess."

"We are. Yet again." He sighed.

Nicolas followed the direction of his gaze. Antonia sat further away, her belly rounded under her muslin dress, chatting with her brother and sister-in-law.

"My darling wife says she will be happy either way," Guy went on, "but I must admit I find myself wishing for a little girl."

Nicolas smiled. Leon had released his leg at least, in favor of sitting at his feet, grabbing handfuls of grass and throwing them in the air.

"I hate to tell you this, but while you might get a Clara, you also might get an Isabella."

Her nodded toward the black-haired little girl who was sitting on the gravel near the steps leading inside the house, trying to pile up rocks, her hair in disarray and her dress covered in dust.

And that was nothing compared to Raoul and Suzanne's girl, who had started to climb walls almost as soon as she'd learned to walk. But no use giving Guy any nightmares.

"I suppose you're right," Guy replied. "Let us pray Antonia safely delivers a healthy baby, that's all that matters. Oh, blast, I think Samuel just poked his brother in the eye with a stick. You really need to teach them how to fight fair while you're here."

"Ha! Since when do I fight fair?"

Guy wandered off toward his sons, and Violette appeared on the path, hurrying toward them, her cheeks flushed. She beamed at him, and his heart bloomed in his chest. No matter how briefly they were parted, no matter if she was close by, seeing her return to his side always filled him with delight.

"Is everything all right?" she asked.

"*Maman!*"

Leon stood up and ran to her, burying himself in her skirts.

"There, my sweet," she said, stroking his hair, then glanced up at Nicolas. "He doesn't want to play with Samuel and his brothers?"

"Not yet, but you know it always takes him time to drop his reserve. He's a bit standoffish, that one." He tapped his chin with his forefinger. "I wonder who he got that particular trait from? A true mystery."

She waved him off but her eyes were shining with amusement. "Hush, you silly man. I just want him to enjoy himself. It would do him good to have fun with other children."

Worry knitted her brow. Bless her, she was always so concerned with what was best for those she loved. Their son, of course, but him as well. Turning their new lodgings on Rivoli street into a home, discussing the management of the gymnasium with him, looking over the accounts—something in which she was so remarkably skilled that he often thought of doing away with his accountant altogether. And supporting him, no matter what.

He stepped closer and cupped her face with his palm. "Be at ease, my love. We'll be here for ten more days. Surrounded by family and friends. Springtime in bloom. What could be better?"

She leaned into his touch. "Nothing, my love. Nothing at all."

THE END

About the Author

Twenty years after studying history at the Sorbonne, Delphine Roy put her classwork to good use in her spicy historical romances set in Post-Revolutionary France. Before that, she spent a good part of her childhood on both sides of the Atlantic and started writing stories in French and English. Her teenage self may have posted them in online fanfiction forums that thankfully no longer exist.

Delphine now lives in the suburbs of Paris with her husband and her son. She's a high school ESL teacher by day and an author by night of romance (in English) and fantasy (in French). In her free time, she enjoys cross-stitching, watching hockey and going down Wikipedia wormholes.